Brokeheart

Brokeheart

KEVIN WOLF

First Edition
First Printing, 2017

Book design by Jake Nordby
Cover design by Nikki Farinella
Cover images by Brenda Timmermans/Pexels; Unsplash/Pexels; Photo Collections/Pexels
Cover title font by Manfred Klein Fonteria

This is a work of fiction. Names, characters, places, and incidents are either the product of the author's imagination or are used fictitiously, and any resemblance to actual persons living or dead, business establishments, events, or locales is entirely coincidental. Cover models used for illustrative purposes only and may not endorse or represent the book's subject.

Library of Congress Cataloging-in-Publication Data (Pending)
978-1-63583-900-5
Library of Congress Control Number: 2017947412

North Star Editions, Inc.
2297 Waters Drive
Mendota Heights, MN 55120
www.northstareditions.com

Printed in the United States of America

For Micah, Lucas, Seth, Porter, and Bode.
And the good things you will do.

Chapter One

1879

The hole wasn't six feet deep. Only paying customers got the full six feet. I threw the last shovels of dirt out of the grave and then used the notch the undertaker had scratched on the handle to measure its depth.

I had jumped down from a freight wagon early that morning. My pockets were empty. A sign in a storefront window offered twenty-five cents to dig the final resting place for some poor soul whose luck had run out.

When I touched the shovel's blade to the bottom of the hole, the mark, halfway up the handle, lined up with the rim of the grave. I'd earned that two bits.

A breeze from the creek bottom tried its best to cool me, but it was a hot breath across my salty skin. My hands found the small of my back. I straightened and scanned the fringe of brush just uphill from the graveyard. Some thought from deep inside my head told me that someone was watching me. But no eyes looked back. Still, that thought hooked its fingernails into my soul like a bad dream that refused to melt away in the daylight.

My shirt and hat hung on a splintered wooden cross a few steps away. I dressed and picked up my carpetbag, tucked the Sharps buffalo gun under my arm, and left the cemetery with the undertaker's shovel over my shoulder.

I'd trade the undertaker his shovel for the money he

owed me. Then I'd find the newspaper office. Word had it that this town might have use for a man of my talents. The cemetery gate squeaked shut behind me, and a coyote's howl answered from the hillside.

Maybe not a coyote. More like a wolf.

Heat as merciless as that on Graveyard Hill made drawing in a breath difficult. Wilson drummed ink-stained fingers on a battered roll-top desk. Drops of sweat shined on the man's bald head. He pivoted in his chair and looked at me.

"Kepler, newspaper men talk among themselves. I know why you need work." He leaned back in his chair.

I curled my lip over my teeth and bit down. Sweat ran down my back. I started to speak but Wilson waved his hand.

"I'm just a printer. When the mine went down ten years ago, this town went bust. I bought this newspaper for a song. Everyone thought I was out of my mind. But I held on."

He jerked his head toward the next room. A black iron press sat silent among stacks of paper. I'd been around newspapers enough to see that while the old machine was not what they were using in Denver, Cheyenne, or Leadville, it was cared for and in good working order.

"It's 1879, man. Things have changed since statehood," Wilson continued. "Brokeheart was made the county seat last April. The mine's working again. New folks are moving in." He pushed gold-rimmed glasses up his nose. A smudge of black ink separated the two little pig eyes that looked up at me. "I can't do it all myself. I need a reporter."

The editor raised an eyebrow, wanting me to say something, but I thought it best to let the conversation pause.

Wilson pushed at his glasses again, then lowered his voice. "I'll pay you six dollars a week."

"The mine pays ten."

"You're no miner."

"There are other papers and other towns."

"But you're here in Brokeheart." His nose wrinkled and the ink in the crevices darkened. "With two bits in your pocket from digging a grave. That won't pay for the train fare to the next town."

Outside, a steam whistle shrieked. Wilson took his watch from the pocket of his vest. He checked the time and tapped the watch on his desk. "Tell you what. Take the six and you can sleep in the room in the back."

"Seven and the room." My eyes held his. "And three in advance."

"You're in no position to bargain. Every reporter I know thinks all the stories come from the bars and bawdy houses on Front Street." He fussed with a stack of papers on the desk. "Six and one in advance. And I'll only try it for a month."

His hand reached into a vest pocket, and he laid a single silver cartwheel in front of me. "Now, the paper comes out at five each day. That mine whistle runs this town. When it blows, the paper must be on the street." He fumbled at his glasses again. "I want your stories on this desk by ten. Three stories each morning. Good penmanship is important. I don't want to guess at what you've written while I'm setting type."

I tucked the silver dollar into my own pocket. "Where can I clean up?"

Wilson lifted himself from the chair. He pointed toward the room at the back. "Put your things away. I'll have my wife fetch a basin and towel. And there's a Chinaman down the block that will boil your shirts. While he's doing your laundry, he'll feed you and get you a bath, if that's what you're wanting."

Eyebrows as bushy as his mustache followed the furrows up his forehead. "I can see where a tall man like you with all that blonde hair might get to thinking he was something special." His voice was low again. "I told you: newspapermen talk. I know what cost you your last job. If you're thinking of messing with my wife, I'll do more than just fire you."

I recalled the whiskers on the chin of the large woman at the desk in the next room. "I've learned my lesson, sir."

"Kepler, I expect your first stories on my desk in the morning."

"Anything in particular you were thinking of, sir?"

He huffed his flabby cheeks. "The murder."

"There was a murder?"

"It's all they're talking about on Front Street. The rabble down there says an evil demon killed him." Wilson leaned toward me. "You're not afraid of spirits, are you?"

I shook my head. "I don't believe in spirits, and I've seen enough of this world to know there's no evil. Just good and bad rolls of the dice." I studied my new employer's face. "When did the murder happen?"

"Just last night. I thought you knew. You dug his grave."

I changed into the cleanest of my dirty white shirts, rolled up the sleeves, and took my trail clothes and other shirts to the Chinaman. Then, with my stomach filled with rice and a dime gone from the two bits I'd earned, I began to explore the town of Brokeheart.

Wilson had pointed out Sheriff Beard's office. Most lawmen in worn-out mine camps welcome the opportunity to talk with a newspaperman. They tell stories of how dangerous their jobs are and how brave they must be. They hope I will weave their lies into the hero's story of some dime novel.

The sheriff's boots rested on the desk, and he tilted back on the rear legs of his chair. A large Bible lay open in his lap. He closed the book and unfolded his long legs.

"Kepler, isn't it?" He stood. "I guessed you'd be down to visit 'fore long."

My mouth opened.

"Wilson sent word with that old Indian." Beard smiled down at me. "If you haven't met Joe yet, you will."

Because of my own stature, I look up to few men. Sheriff Beard towered a full head above me.

He placed the Bible on his desk. "Welcome to Brokeheart, Mr. Kepler."

"It's Kepler. Just Kepler. No mister."

"Kepler your first name or your last name?"

"Neither."

He started to speak, when a voice came from behind a thick wooden door at the rear of his office.

"Parson?" The tone was weak.

The big lawman nodded for me to follow. "We're comin', Cap'n." Then to me, "You'll want to talk to the captain. He's the witness to our little murder."

The way he said "little murder" made death sound insignificant. Life and death in these boomtowns often was.

"Did I hear him call you 'Parson'?"

The sheriff smiled. "I preach the Sunday meetin's at the Baptist church."

The captain huddled on an iron cot behind the open door of an otherwise empty cell. Despite the heat of the afternoon, I was sure I saw the man shiver. He looked up at us with eyes as milky as opals.

The sheriff hooked his finger in the iron bars and nodded. "The captain here was at the top of the hill when Pickett sent his boys up the ridge the last day of Gettysburg. Ain't that right?"

The old man straightened his back, and a smile curled across his face, exposing toothless gums. "Sixth New York Artillery." Gnarled fingers touched his eyebrow in a half salute. "We gave them Rebs double canister at ten yards."

In that instant, his pride in whatever he had done that day chased away the years of rotgut whiskey and black-pit mining.

"We held our ground. We surely did."

"That's right, Cap'n." The sheriff used his pastoral voice. "Now, tell Kepler here about what you saw in the alley last night."

The soldier's ramrod in the captain's back crumbled in a dozen places, and he slumped forward. Bony hands pushed back his hair, and he shivered again.

"An angel."

"Tell 'im, Cap'n."

"An angel. Dressed all in white. Dark hair a-flowin'." The captain tugged at the front of his shirt. "But it weren't no angel. Standin' over Jeff. Drippin' his blood from her lips. And I heard her scream." The captain's chin dropped onto his chest and he began to sob.

"Get some sleep, Cap'n. The Chinaman's gonna bring your food 'fore long. Rest up, hear me?" Beard motioned toward the door, and I followed him back to his office. "He started talkin' about an angel drippin' blood and got a bunch of drunks laughin' at him. The more they laughed, the more he swore it was true. I thought it best for him to rest here for a day or two."

"You don't believe him?"

"Would you? The man's half-blind." The sheriff dropped into his chair. "The captain has had a life full of what this town was named for. Now he swamps out the Months Saloon for the pennies the girls give 'im. Empties spittoons and mucks out the privy. And he'll lick out what's left in the glasses if the girls don't catch him. No, I don't believe 'im."

"Then what happened to this Jeff?"

The lawman ran his hand across the stubble on his chin. "Jeff got busted up in an accident over at the mine ten to twelve years ago. He was 'bout as bad off as the cap'n. The mine let 'im sleep in a shack over there. Gave him a few cents a month to run errands." He nodded for me to sit, but I shook my head.

"I think old Jeff got a little too much whiskey in him. Railroaders were drinkin' up their paychecks. Somebody bought him a few. He staggered out into the alley to sleep it off. Slipped, fell, and hit his head. Cap'n found 'im."

"What about the blood he said he saw?"

"Oh, there was blood, all right. The ground was still wet with it." The sheriff tapped his temple. "A gash in his head. I think some coyotes wandered into town and got to his throat and face 'fore we found 'im in the mornin'."

"You didn't find him until morning? Wasn't it some time at night when the captain saw the . . . angel?"

Beard shook his head. "But no one believed 'im. The cap'n tells a lot of stories. So no one thought anythin' of it." He tapped his fingers on the Bible on his desk. "Tell you what, meet me an hour after dark tonight. I'm goin' to take a scattergun and lantern over to that alley. If that angel coyote is thinkin' 'bout comin' 'round again, I'll pepper his butt. It'll give me a chance to introduce ya to the folks you should know on Front Street."

Chapter Two

I left the sheriff's office and let the toes of my boots lead me down the boardwalks of Main Street. I wanted to visit the Months Saloon on my own. Barroom conversations would be more forthcoming without the big lawman at my side.

Women in their summer bonnets strolled by, keeping to the little shade afforded by the false fronts of the buildings. A team of horses pulling a farm wagon stirred fine dust into the still air. Hot sunlight sparkled off the suspended grit.

Where the boardwalk ended, I turned west toward Front Street. New, white-washed buildings gave way to a block of shacks and empty corrals. I dodged a wagon and team, then crossed the rutted street to the saloon.

Hemp twine tied back the front doors. Three workers in railroad stripes shared a table. Rough-cut planks nailed to empty beer barrels made the bar.

"We don't get many white shirts in here." The folds of flesh on the arms of the woman behind the bar swung in the same cadence as the newspaper she used for a fan. "You Kepler? Word's already out 'bout ya."

"Is the beer warm?"

"Sugar, on a day like this it's almost hot."

"Got any good whiskey?"

"Ain't had good whiskey in the ten years I've run the place." Powdered jowls and extra chins framed what had once been a compact face. Gaudy red daubed her cheeks and lips. Limp, dark hair fell to the apron tied at her thick waist. "No un's gone blind from this batch. That's as good as whiskey gets in this place."

Over the bar, a dusty, faded painting of another woman stared at the saloon floor. The woman in the portrait was younger, slimmer, and naked, but as worn-looking as the real woman in front of me.

"I'm May." She took the stub of a cigar from a fold in her dress and hung it in the corner of her mouth. She put down her fan and struck a match with her thumbnail. "That ain't me in the picture, case you're wonderin'." She sucked the flame into the tobacco. "It was here when I bought the place. Old-timers tell me her name was June. Been a lot of other Junes since her."

"Will I find a card game here tonight?"

May nodded toward a backroom. "Liquor up front." Smoke curled from her lips. "Poker in the rear."

I fought the smile that tightened my face.

"Hankerin' for one of the girls?" May blew gray smoke in my face.

"Not now. But I will have some bad whiskey."

"The first one's on me. And play your cards down the street. This here's a workin' man's bar. I ain't gonna let them men lose what few cents they got to the likes of you." She wiped out a glass with a rag and then sloshed two fingers of whiskey into it. "Why ya in here, Kepler?"

"Tell me about Jeff."

"Like, do I believe an angel kilt him?"

Turpentine fumes stung my nose as I tilted the dirty glass to my lips. The whiskey burned down and sent hot fumes back up. My lungs found breath again. "I'll pay for the next." I coughed and May laughed.

Just then, the sound of men's voices came down the street. The railroaders hurried from their table. The men outside shouted, and I could make out a few words of Spanish from a high-pitched voice.

"Muerta . . . Agua . . . Mujer . . . Muerta."

Then a loud voice yelled out, "This pepper-belly sez there's a dead woman down by the creek."

Another voice called, "Git the sheriff."

I hurried out onto the street. Behind me, May shouted up the stairs for her girls. I jostled my way into the group of a dozen men and followed them around the side of the Months Saloon. We crossed a narrow alley that separated the buildings on Front Street from a row of slanting shacks and cabins at the top of the steep creek bank.

A burly, red-bearded teamster pushed a dark-skinned boy ahead of him. "Show us where ya saw her, Paco."

Below the cutbank, the aspen trees on the hillside blended into a tangle of old cottonwoods and willows. Weeds, gone brown from the summer heat, wove a thick carpet along the stream. Through the maze of branches, sunlight reflected back in specks and spots from the water. I squinted into the brush, trying to spot the body.

"*Aquí, aquí,*" the Mexican pointed.

Red-whiskers clamped a handful of the kid's shirt in his big fist. "Where, damn it?" He shook the kid like a rag doll. "I don't see nothin'."

As those words left his mouth, an axe handle tapped the teamster's wrist.

"Let the boy go." Sheriff Beard pushed the blunt end

of the handle under Red's chin. He snatched the kid around the waist, and the two jumped down into the creek bottom.

I hopped off the edge. My boots caught in the soft dirt and I pitched forward, scrambling to keep my feet under me.

"I see her, Paco," Sheriff Beard said.

I studied the grass and branches in front of me. Not finding anything, I turned to the sheriff and the Mexican.

Paco made the sign of the cross. "*Madre de Dios.*" He pointed at the largest cottonwood.

The sheriff turned his head to me. "She's in the tree." He stabbed the axe handle into soft mud at the edge of the creek and then splashed into the water.

I shaded my eyes and looked into the branches. Not finding anything, I followed. Creek water lapped over my boots and my feet made sucking noises when I pulled them out of the mud. A breath of breeze puffed at the cottonwoods' leaves. A shape twisted ever so slightly. I heard the flies, and then in the shadows I saw the woman twisting at the end of a rope.

I slogged out of the water and kicked though the tangles to join the sheriff. Paco backed away. He turned when he reached the stream and ran. Beard said nothing. His chin dropped to his chest, and he clamped his eyes shut. I guessed the parson-sheriff was praying.

His eyes opened and he whispered to me, "Fifth one this year."

"What?"

"Miner's wife. Suicide." His head shook slowly. "One of ya go tell Madison at the mine office and send somebody to find the undertaker," he called to the mob that had followed to the far bank of the stream.

Two men peeled away from the group. One headed toward the mine, the other toward town. The rest stayed on the other side of the little river. None of them spoke. May came down the hill, pushed her way through, lifted her skirt, and slogged into the water.

"Help me get her down." The sheriff's words made my stomach turn.

She was tiny, not much bigger than a child. Her feet hung a foot off the ground. Black flies swarmed over her face. A swollen, waxy, blue tongue covered with the insects stuck from her mouth. Blood stained the collar of a threadbare dress. One shoe clung to a foot, the other lost somewhere in the weeds.

"Get 'er ankles." Beard took a knife from his boot, reached up and cut the rope above her long, dark hair.

I stepped closer and caught her bare legs. The touch of her skin chilled me, and sickness boiled in my stomach.

As gently as we could, we laid her on the grass.

"Look at 'er throat." The sheriff licked his lips. "Put 'er head in the noose but didn't weigh enough to snap her neck. Hung there clawin' at 'er throat while she strangled."

"How long . . . er, when do you think it happened?"

"I'm guessin' sometime late last night."

"Poor thing." May knelt down and whisked the flies away. "Came all the way across the ocean. Married off to some man she hardly knew. Thought she was in America and everythin' would be better." May lifted a long, silver chain from the dead woman's collar and placed the cross between the woman's breasts. "She found herself in Brokeheart, and this was 'er only way out."

May untied her apron and spread it over the glazed eyes and protruding tongue. Black flies buzzed all around us.

"Judas Priest!" a new voice called. A short, wiry man splashed at edge of the stream. The man stopped and put both hands on his hips. "This is gonna cost me a whole day of production at the mine."

May whirled around and pointed a finger at him. "This girl died here, Madison. And yer worried 'bout losin' money!"

The sheriff pulled May back and said something to her I couldn't make out.

"Do you want to look at 'er, Madison?" Beard asked. "See if you know who she is?"

The man stayed rooted where he stood. "I wouldn't recognize her." He dropped his hands and balled them into fists. "I'll send Giuseppe to look at her. He can tell her kin when they come up from the mine. Let the undertaker know I'll take care of things, like before. Bury her tomorrow. I don't want this to drag out."

"That's big of you, Madison." May tried to push around the sheriff but he caught a fold in her dress and pulled her back.

Madison shook his head. "You know these people. They'll make a party of this thing, cry and carry on. Judas Priest." He turned and sloshed away back down the stream.

May, Beard, and I stood by the body for a moment more. I swatted a blowfly that landed on the back of my hand. A tear ran down May's cheek.

An Indian with a face as wrinkled as a dried apple motioned to the sheriff from where he knelt by the stream's edge. I followed Beard through the weeds. The Indian pointed at marks in the mud.

The sheriff squatted and touched the tracks. "Big coyote. Near as big as a wolf. Probably smelled her blood."

He stood up and spoke to the Indian. "Joe, you stay with her body 'til the undertaker gets here. Keep everybody away, hear me?"

We went back to May. The minister part of the sheriff touched her shoulder. "Nothin' more we can do here."

She pushed his hand away and left us without speaking. The big woman waded through creek, pushed aside the men who had gathered, and marched up the hill.

"Sheriff, where did they find Jeff's body?" I asked.

"Right up there. Behind May's saloon. In the alleyway."

I looked at the piece of rope still swinging from the tree, then back to where the sheriff had pointed. "Remember what the captain said about the angel? Dressed in white? Long, black hair? Dripping blood? Do you think he might have seen her hanging here?"

Beard pulled up the axe handle from the mud and tapped the toe of his boot. "Full moon last night, bright enough someone might just be able to see. If he knew where to look. But Cap'n's near blind."

Dread pulled my eyes back to the dead woman. I was thankful that May had covered her face.

"First Jeff, then this 'un." The sheriff tucked the axe handle under his arm. "Somethin' else is bound to happen. Bad comes in threes."

Chapter Three

Rust-colored ants and shiny black beetles swarmed over the blood-soaked dirt where Jeff's body had lain. From the alley, I looked down to the creek bottom where Indian Joe squatted in a patch of shade a dozen paces from the woman's body, waiting for the undertaker. The sheriff was right. The tangle of limbs and weeds where the woman had died would be hard to spot.

If I took two steps up the alley, I could make out the rope that she'd hung from, still tied to a twisted branch. But this was afternoon and the captain had seen his angel after midnight. Even if a full moon lit the night, I doubted if anyone, let alone a half-blind old man, would be able to make out that terrible place beside the creek.

A yellow cat scampered across the alley and leaped on the porch at the back of May's saloon. A girl in a red dress scooped it up and nuzzled the animal's face with her own.

"Why ya lookin' at that place, mister?"

She was no more than sixteen. The sun had bleached her hair to the color of corn silk. Freckles splashed across her nose. Bright red makeup that matched her dress spread over her lips. She leaned on the door frame and crossed one bare foot over the other.

"I wanted to see where they found Jeff."

Her mouth trembled. "This here's Mr. Buggs." She hugged the cat tighter. "I named him that 'cause he eats

’em. You know, bugs.” She nodded at the insects on the stained soil. “What’s your name, Mister?”

“People call me Kepler.”

“They call me June. I’m one of Miss May’s girls.”

“May told me that June was the name of the girl in the picture over the bar.”

“There’s been seven–maybe eight–Junes ’twixt her and me. June ain’t my real name. Miss May says nobody cares about a whore’s real name.”

“What should I call you, then?”

“Call me June. I’ll call you Kepler.” She kissed the top of the cat’s head. “Men in the bar sayin’ a lady kilt herself down there. That true?”

“I’m afraid so.”

“I heard her scream out last night.” One hand held the cat, the other twisted a strand of her white-blond hair in her fingers. I moved closer to the door where she stood. Suddenly June pushed the yellow cat away from her so that it dangled from her outstretched arms. Her fingers wrapped around Mr. Buggs’ neck and she began to squeeze. The animal yowled. Its teeth and claws raked the girl’s arms.

“June!”

Her eyes squeezed into tight slits, staring at the struggling animal, blood welling in her scratches.

I grabbed June’s arms and tried to pry her fingers apart. The hard muscles in June’s wrists refused to loosen. As suddenly as it had all began, her grip relaxed. Mr. Buggs dropped to the splintered floor and dashed into the weeds along the alley.

June tilted her face up at me. The freckles on her nose wrinkled and she smiled. “Miss May don’t let jus’ anybody go upstairs with me. Bet she’d let you, Kepler.”

Notes played on an out-of-tune piano drifted from the saloon. June shook free of my hands.

"Be sure to speak with Miss May," she said over her shoulder as she stepped through the door into the Months Saloon.

Sweat streamed down my face and I slumped against the rough board siding. My tongue stuck to the roof of my mouth as my brain tried to sort out these strange events.

What tormented June so? Was it the same anguish that I had seen in the captain? Had some evil angel visited this place? One thing I was sure of: a woman choking at the end of a rope could not scream out.

The yellow cat stalked to the edge of the weeds and studied the teeming insects. Lightning quick, it pounced. Mr. Buggs plucked a carrion beetle from the bloody dirt.

Chapter Four

I hurried from the heat and dust of Front Street to the heat and dust of the boardwalks on Main Street. Questions in the pit of my stomach pulled me to the undertaker's.

"Hello?" I called, stepping from the sun into the cramped shop.

"Ain't cuttin' hair today." The words came from behind a black curtain that separated the room with the barber chair from a small alcove. "Jesus, Mary, and Joseph. Come back tomorrow afternoon. I gots two funerals in the morning."

"It's not about a haircut. Could I . . ."

Stubby fingers pulled at the side of the curtains and a little man limped out. He hooked his thumbs in the front of his pants and tugged them up his fleshy stomach. Tightly rolled rags hung from his nostrils.

"It's you. Heard you're a reporter now. Wilson ain't payin' you?" One finger dug into his ear. "Lookin' for another two bits?"

"I'm not here to dig a grave."

"Then what?"

"Could I see Jeff's body?"

The undertaker pulled the finger from his ear and squinted at whatever was stuck to the tip. "Why?" He wiped the finger on his pants. "Jeff didn't smell good when he was alive. He's been in that back shed all day. In this heat, he's startin' to ripen up. If'n you want to see a dead 'un," he whispered, "I'll let you take a peek at the woman they brought in." One eyebrow arched. "She's a pretty one. And still fresh."

I shook my head.

He shrugged and pointed to long strips of cloth on a table near the curtain. "Roll 'em up and stuff 'em in tight." He tapped his own nose. "Stops that perfumery smell some." He grinned.

I took the material and wadded it tightly. "When is Jeff's funeral?"

"Early tomorrow. Before the other." He paced in front of the curtain. "Sheriff'll read over him. Not much of a funeral.

"There'll be a crowd for hers. It'll be strange, though."

"How's that?"

"She kilt herself!" He pushed back a worn derby hat, exposing his scaly, bald scalp. "Otherwise they'd be buryin' her in the graveyard by the Catholic church." He tugged one rag out of his nose then the other. "Folks will cry and carry on somethin' fierce. But hardly any will come in the graveyard fence. Suicide's a mortal sin, ya know." His eyes rolled back.

"Is that how it was with the others?"

"Others?"

"Beard told me that there were other suicides."

"Not the men. But them miner folk get mighty agitated about the women. Should'a heard the wailin' over the little girl."

"A little girl killed herself?"

"No!" He pulled the derby back in place. "Mother took

a knife to the child, then killed herself. Just out beyond the roundhouse. Never seen so much blood."

"Tell me about the others."

"What others?" He rubbed his face.

"Suicides. What happened with them?"

"An old miner down on his luck told the boys at the bar he was gonna end it all. Everybody thought he'd just had too much of May's whiskey. We picked up what was left of him off'n the tracks. Engineer said the fella jumped in front of the train."

"When was that?

"Same day we found the woman and her girl. There was still snow in the shadows of the buildings. I'm guessin' two months ago."

I pulled in a breath. "That's four. The sheriff said that the woman this morning was the fifth."

"Yep. The woman who kilt her daughter, the husband put a shotgun to his head that night. I got paid good for them." He scratched at his ear again. "You gonna look at Jeff or keep me gabbin' so I can't get any work done?"

He pushed me out a door to the packed-dirt yard behind the store. One shed was filled with boards and tools for new caskets. The other held Jeff.

The stream of sunlight through the door made the only light. The man's body stretched out on a low table that filled the room. Floating dust peppered the air. A sour stench seeped around the rags in my nose.

I pulled away the feed sacks that covered the corpse. Skin had peeled away from a gash on the forehead. Bone glistened like new ivory. A spider's web of sticky black blood covered the man's face. A lump rose in my throat. I swallowed hard to fight back the taste of bile.

The sheriff's words about animals tearing at the face and neck should have prepared me. The dead man's lower lip, wrenched away from his face, hung like butcher's meat. Skin and muscle had been peeled back from below one ear to the collar bone. Blue veins and white tendons shined from the glaze of the heat.

Despite the carnage, my eyes locked on the gouges in the skin of the dead man's throat. The marks were evenly spaced from his chin to the collar of his frayed shirt. I had seen similar scratches a few hours earlier—above the bloodstains on the worn dress of the woman hanging from the tree limb.

I folded the burlap back over Jeff's mangled face and left the shed. The smell of death oozed into the pores of my skin and I felt its invisible stains on my clothes.

The sound of a hammer driving nails into soft pine echoed across the undertaker's yard. I slipped back in through the shop's door and pulled back the black curtain to the niche where the woman's body lay. Shadowy light played over her frail body. I snapped my fist to my mouth and bit into the soft place at the base of my thumb. The sinful troll of a man had stripped off the woman's dress and underthings. A new bedsheet covered her legs and hips. Sightless eyes stared at the ceiling. A single deerfly perched on a wrinkled gray nipple. Blue veins laced skin as pale as candle wax.

Shame made me grind my teeth harder into my hand. Slowly, I forced my eyes to look at her throat. It was as I remembered. Below the bruise from the rope, distinct slashes ripped across each side of her neck. The sheriff had said that she had clawed at her own throat as she strangled.

Her hands lay at her sides, covered by the rough cloth.

The sound of my own heart pumped in my ears. Outside, I heard the vile little man curse. I tugged the cloth back and leaned closer. The nails showed the marks of scrubboards and lye soap. But there was not a sign of blood on her fingers.

I replaced the cloth over her hands and shooed the fly away from her. I hurried away, through the curtain and out onto the street. My fingers pulled at the buttons on my shirt. I let the hot afternoon breeze wash over my bare chest, wishing that it would clean the deathly smell off my body and away from my soul.

My pace quickened until I stepped through the door of the Chinaman's. I tossed a few pennies onto the counter and stripped off the shirt.

There are occasions when a man's devotion to his trade becomes its own reward. The clang of a blacksmith's hammer turns to song. Sweat falls from a farmer's face to water his crops. Chips drop away and a woodcarver's vision takes shape.

That evening as I put pen to paper, I wrote as I had few times before.

My first story for the *Brokeheart Gazette* would tell about the scene beside the stream. My mind had memorized the noise of the flies, the stifling heat, and the woman's grotesque mask of death. One shoe on. One shoe lost. New rope tied to the crooked tree limb. A doll's crumpled body resting in brown weeds, covered with a bar-woman's stained apron. As the lantern flickered on the desk beside me, I found the words to tell others of the cool, dead flesh I had touched.

I did not write of a defeated woman, but of a new angel freed from the disappointment of her earthly bonds.

Chapter Five

The clock on the newspaper office wall chimed at nine thirty. With a last stroke of my pen, I signed my name and then blotted the paper. I placed the two stories on my employer's desk: a few brief paragraphs concerning Jeff's body in the alley and the effortless composition on the nameless woman.

While I was writing, a place in my mind had reviewed the things I saw at the undertaker's. Two bodies awaiting morning funerals. I recalled the parson-sheriff's declaration that "bad comes in threes."

The heat of the day faded with the sunlight. The evening chose shades of deep blues and gray to paint over the shops and streets of Brokeheart. I took a small Smith and Wesson revolver from my carpetbag, checked to be sure the cylinder was still loaded, and then tucked it into the waistband of my trousers. I slid into a canvas trail jacket and left the office for the meeting with Sheriff Beard.

Just a thumbnail-width was missing from last night's full moon. Yellow lights flickered in the windows of the homes on the hill. The storefronts all along Main Street sat dark and locked. A mile away, a bonfire lit the evening near the miners' shacks across the creek from where the woman had hung.

Men's voices from the sheriff's office carried on the still air. I hopped up from the street onto the boardwalk and reached for the door handle. The door swung open before my hand found the latch. A man's head and shoulders filled the frame.

"No." The man turned to the sheriff. "No matter what you say you saw there, I won't believe Sophia could do such a thing." The man shook his head and turned to leave. A white collar circled his neck above the top of his dark clothes. He lifted a black hat and was about to place it on his head when he saw me.

The sheriff said to me, "Tell the Father what we saw down at the creek." Then to the priest, "Kepler helped me cut her down." Beard leaned a hip onto his desk. "Kepler, meet Father Dowd. He's the priest here in town."

Father Dowd took my hand, but his attention stayed on the sheriff. "Sophia left the church last night after ten. She was happy and smiling. She had no reason to take her own life."

I whispered, "At the undertaker's . . ." Neither man looked my way.

"You are depriving her of a burial at the church." The priest stared down the sheriff.

I put my arm out to stop the priest. "You don't understand." Ignoring me, he stepped just outside the office door into the night air.

"Father, at the undertaker's, I saw Sophia's body . . ." I could not make the words come.

His hand made the sign of the cross. "Please let her rest in peace."

"She hung herself." Beard's voice was calm. "Until we find some proof otherwise, that's it."

"Then stop the funeral." Dowd slapped his fist in his hand.

"That's Madison's call."

"He's only concerned with making money," the priest said. "He wants the funeral tomorrow because the mine works half days on Saturdays. He's giving the miners a half day off instead of a full day. And he hopes they forget about all this by Monday."

Beard looked at the floor between his boots. "There's nothing I can do."

The muscles in Dowd's jaws worked in and out. Then he strode off down the dark street.

"Dagnabbit," Beard whispered. He pinched the bridge of his nose between his calloused fingers.

Beard picked a folded paper from beside his open Bible. "Got something for you. The Indian left it for me to give to you."

He handed me a piece of fine, new stationery. It was folded into thirds and sealed with red wax.

I tore it open and tilted the page so I could read from the light of the coal-oil lamp on Beard's desk.

Kepler,
I have a business proposition I would like to discuss.
Please come to my private car in the railyard.
I have other business that will encumber me until
midnight. I must see you. Come at one a.m.

There was no signature, only an ornate coat of arms at the letterhead. In the dim light I could not make out the decoration's intricate design.

"What ya got there, Kepler?"

"An invitation to meet the owner of that railroad car you told me about. He wants to meet at one o'clock." I paused, then added, "Tonight."

The sheriff cocked his head. "Strange."

I stuffed the letter into a jacket pocket. "Yes, very strange. But it might make a good story."

Beard shrugged his rounded shoulders. "Let's take a walk down to Front Street." He took a long coat from a peg on the wall and put it on. "It's quiet down there tonight. No rail crews in town. Dowd said the bunch from the mine is havin' some sorta wake for the woman. Sophia Martelli, I think he said her name was."

"I saw Sophia's body at the undertaker's."

"Ya heard the priest. Best leave it be." Beard looked me over slowly. "Town's got an ordinance 'bout carryin' firearms." He nodded at the bulge at my waist. "What you got there?"

I pulled back my jacket until the butt of the pistol showed.

"Pretty little thing." He held out his hand. "Where'd you get that?"

"It was a gift." I took the weapon from my belt and held it in my open palm.

"Nickel-plated." Beard lifted the gun from my hand. "Pearl handles. Engraved. A hide-out piece, huh? Looks like somethin' a Denver sporting-house lady'd keep in her garter."

He handed it back grips first.

"My mother gave it to me."

"Kepler, sometimes I don't know how to take you." He lifted a long-barreled shotgun from a set of deer antlers on the wall. "Don't make a habit of carryin' that thing."

He picked up a lantern and I followed him out the door.

May sat on a sagging chair outside her saloon. The same folded newspaper she had used for a fan that afternoon now swatted at the gnats that strayed from the swarm near the lighted windows.

Down Front Street, near the railyards, I heard a horse snort. The piano in May's was quiet. The sheriff, May, and I were the only ones on the street.

"Peaceful." The big woman leaned back in the chair. "Shh, now listen. June's out back a-singin' to her cat."

A childlike voice drifted through the night air—a lullaby of butterflies, midnight ladies, and circus colors.

May smiled. Her eyes closed. "Sometimes it does a body good to forget."

The cool night made me want to forget. But too many thoughts raced in my mind.

"Ya boys et?" May asked. "April traded a cowboy for a string of trout. June picked some greens down 'long the creek.

April's gonna cook 'em up. Cap'n's inside a-helpin' her. 'Nuff for ya if ya want. Don't look like we'll be doin' much business tonight."

The sheriff nodded.

May hoisted herself from the old chair. "I'll have April fix ya both a plate. C'mon in when you hear us holler. We won't wait."

A dog's bark broke the stillness. June's song stopped and the burros in the mine's corrals put up a ruckus. The dog's bark turned to a yowl and several other curs joined in. On the creek bottom, a coyote howled. Then everything went quiet again. "Might be that coyote that tore up Jeff." Beard broke open the shotgun and dropped a shell in each barrel. "Let's ease around back and see if we can get a shot.

Birdshot in its behind might make it realize it ain't welcome." He put a match to the railroad lantern and handed the light to me.

We crept along the side of the saloon, crossed the alleyway and slipped between the abandoned shacks above the creek bed. Our boots crunched gravel, and water gurgled in the creek below us. Silvery moonlight floated over our heads but failed to penetrate the dark tangle of brush and trees in the wash. Beard nodded and raised the shotgun to his shoulder. I pulled up the brass cover from the lantern and swung a beam of harsh yellow light along the edge of the weeds. Birds' wings rustled and a dozen took flight.

At the edge of the thicket, a set of eyes glowed red in the light. Beard thumbed back the hammers on his scattergun. The metal click sent the animal scrambling away from us.

I lifted the lantern higher, trying to light whatever moved.

Footsteps splashed in the creek, and in the blend of lantern light and moonbeams I saw a woman. Her white gown flowed behind her as she darted away through the trees.

"No," I shouted, "don't shoot."

"I see it." Beard lowered his gun. "Must be June chasing her cat."

"Those weren't cat eyes shinin'. And the girl would have called out."

Even as I said it, I doubted. I remembered June squeezing the neck of her cat that afternoon and wondered if she really would have called to us.

From the darkness of the alley behind us, a strained voice whispered, "Help me."

The sheriff snatched the lantern from my hand and

hurried between the empty cabins to the back of May's. Shotgun in one hand and light held high in the other, he scanned the alley. I was two steps behind him.

At the edge of the circle of light, a man sprawled on the ground. He tried to raise an arm but the effort was too much and his hand fell to the dust beside him.

"Sheriff."

"I see 'im."

The globe of yellow light bounced over the rutted path as the sheriff hurried to the figure in the dirt. The man croaked out a few words and the sheriff knelt down.

"It's all right, Captain," he said, touching the man's face. Then to me, "Get May."

May and June came through the saloon's door into the alley. May waddled over to the sheriff and the man on the ground. The freckles on June's nose wrinkled and the moonlight sparkled on her teeth. She caught me by the arm and pulled close to me.

The front of the captain's shirt shone black with blood. His head twitched and then slumped to the side. The sheriff's back straightened and his head bowed.

"Poor old man," May cried. "Your tough life's over, Cap'n."

I bent forward and tugged at his shirt collar. In the dim light cast by the lantern, I saw the captain's throat was torn away. Evenly spaced marks were clawed into his cheek, and his jaw still oozed blood. I whirled to my feet and caught June by her wrists. I pulled her hands into the light.

Her fingers were clean. There was no blood.

June's head fell back and laughter cascaded out.

As my hands gripped the dead man's ankles, I felt the warmth that had been his life ebb away. In the Months's shadowy back room, we laid the captain's limp body on the dusty floor between barrels of beer and empty whiskey cases.

"Get me more light," Beard said.

May hurried out and returned with a coal-oil lamp in each of her thick hands. A woman with skin the color of muddy coffee and a halo of kinky black curls followed May. The woman stole a glance at the captain's body, covered her mouth with both hands, and looked away.

June's eyes never moved from the old man's torn face and neck. The fingers of one hand tangled in her fine blond hair. Her tongue traced her upper lip.

"He's tore up like Jeff." Beard squatted beside the corpse. He looked up. "What was he doin' in the alley, April?" he asked the black woman.

She turned her face. A shiny pink scar slashed from the center of her forehead, across one eye and down her cheek. A thick film covered the damaged eye. Her body trembled and she chewed at the sleeve of her faded dress.

"Answer the man," May told her.

"I sent him for mo' firewood, dat's all." The words spilled in a slur of sobs. "Den I heard dose dogs a-yappin'."

"Got a blanket we can cover him with?" the sheriff asked.

April nodded and rushed from the room.

"June, were you out back just now?" Beard asked.

Her face twisted and she looked at him with eyes that fought to focus. She shook her head. "Was on the back stoop with Mr. Buggs."

"You weren't down by the creek?" he asked.

"No, sir."

"It wasn't June," I said. "Look at her dress." She was in the same red dress she'd worn that afternoon. "The woman we saw wore white."

Beard pursed his lips. His tongue drew a circle on the inside of his cheek. "I ain't sure what I saw, but no person did this to him." He tipped his head towards the dead man. "Last summer a coyote come into a farmyard on the edge of town and tore into a man's milk cow. The man kilt it with a hatchet when it came after him. Decided it must have had hydrophobie." He looked at the body. "Rabies is about the only thing that would make an animal crazy enough to come into town. Could be what the dogs heard."

"What about what we saw?" I stood up from the floor.

The sheriff's head drooped and his voice rose. "No woman did this." He looked up at me. "I don't care what we saw . . . or think we saw. Some kinda animal ripped this man's throat out."

"But, Sheriff–"

"No." His hands pushed on the dirty floor and he stood up. His eyes locked on mine. "I ain't goin' to let you get this town riled up over some made-up goblin story." The big man pulled his shoulders back. "We're gonna wrap the captain up and bury him with Jeff in the mornin'. As far as anybody knows, his old heart just played out. Understand?"

I held his stare.

"Understand me, Kepler?" he repeated.

I pursed my lips and nodded. I chose not to speak until I could talk with the sheriff alone.

April came back into the room.

May took the worn blanket from her and spread it

over the captain. "I understand. My girls won't say nothin' neither."

The coal-oil lanterns that had lit the poor captain's wake sat side by side on the makeshift kitchen table. April placed plates of limp dandelion greens and barely warm trout in front of each of us. The sheriff folded his hands and bowed his head. His red-rimmed eyes stared at the food. Without a word, he left the plate on the table and stalked from the room.

There was little taste in my first mouthful. The only noises as we ate came from forks touching the plates. June fidgeted in her chair. She shot quick glances at April.

May stood up from the table. "I'll check on the sheriff," she said. "Could use a whiskey."

"I'll have one, too," I told her.

As soon as May left the room, June caught hold of April's dress. "I need—" she whispered.

Frizzy black hair shook. "You's had 'nuff."

"Please." The word whined like a hurt puppy.

"Not now."

"I need it." June's hands caught April's sleeve. "Please."

April reached into a dress pocket under her apron and took out a small, brown glass bottle.

June snatched it from her hand and pulled out the cork stopper. She tilted the bottle back and gulped.

"'Nuff, chile," April said through clenched teeth.

A smile spread on June's face. She wiped her lips with her hand and then licked each finger.

May shuffled into the room. April grabbed the bottle and tried to hide it.

The big woman slammed the whiskey bottle onto the table. Her hand cracked across April's face. "I seen that," she screamed. "I told you never. *Never* give that to the girl."

April shrank back. Her hand touched the spreading welt on her cheek. She tried to speak, but May cut her off. "Give it to me."

June stood quickly and held the back of her chair with both hands. The side of her face dropped onto her shoulder, as if she were bracing for May to slap her next.

May plucked the bottle from April's fist. She caught June's chin in her fingers and tilted the girl's face toward hers. The harshness in her voice softened. "No, my little June." Gentle fingers touched June's freckled cheeks. "Laudanum can only make the hurt go away for very few minutes. When it comes back, it comes back hard. And ya need more. And more after that."

The tip of May's fingers grazed June's forehead. Her thick hand pulled out the bottle's cork and she poured the sticky liquid on the floor. She caught June's shoulders and pulled the frail girl to her bulky body. The other hand caught April's curls. April's face leaned on May's hip. The scarred black woman, the tormented child, and May all began to cry.

"There, there," May said softly.

I was an intruder there, and I left the room.

Sheriff Beard straddled May's chair on the street in front of the saloon, his coat bundled around him in the night chill. His head bowed and the skin around his closed eyes pulled tight in crow's-foot creases.

He raised his face when he heard me.

"You were praying?" I asked.

"Yup." He studied the dark street. "I was prayin' I did the right thing. And prayin' for this town, May and her girls. You, too, Kepler."

I bit my tongue. "You sure that May won't say anything about the captain?"

His legs stretched forward. "May'll keep quiet, if for no other reason than it's good for her business. Talk of murders in the alley might send the miners and rail hands down the street to one of the saloons near the depot. May'll explain it to her girls and they'll do as she says. It's you I'm worrin' about." He tipped the brim of his hat back so that I could see his face in the moonlight. "What's it goin' to be?"

I let out a deep breath. "What would I tell?" My back leaned against the building. "It seems like years ago that I saw something what I thought was a woman running away along the stream. And only for a second. I did see an old man's throat tore to bits. I'm sure of that." I fumbled with the buttons on my jacket.

Beard shook his head. "Look, we went out there sure we was gonna see a coyote. Things happened. Your eyes can play tricks on you. Makes things seem different from what they are. Maybe it was an old barn owl that went swoopin' through those trees. Who knows?"

"I went to the undertaker this afternoon." I couldn't look at him. "Those marks on the captain's neck? There were ones just like 'em on Jeff and the woman we found in the tree. A story like that needs to be told. I'm just not sure now's the right time."

He turned away and I heard him suck a breath through his teeth. "Try prayin'."

"I've tried everything, Sheriff. I've drank whiskey

until I staggered. I've won and lost it all again on the Faro table. Whored." I looked up at the moon. "Tried religion. I prayed like the preacher told me, but in the end it seemed I was the only one that could make things any different."

"Kepler." The sheriff stood up. "There was a man that needed to dig a well so's his wife and children could have water. Every mornin', he went out with a pick and shovel and dug through rocks and dry dirt. End of the week, still no water and he was near twenty feet down. He'd bust the dirt, shovel it into buckets, climb out, and hoist the buckets up at the end of a rope. Then he'd go back down in the hole and do it all again."

Beard picked up his shotgun from where it leaned on the wall. "From the bottom of that dry hole, he looked up at Heaven and told the Good Lord that if he jus' found water, he'd quit all his sinful ways. He meant every word he said." Beard tucked the shotgun into the crook of his elbow. "On the very next swing of his pickax, water started bubblin' into the hole. He looked back up to Heaven and told the Lord, 'Forget all I just promised, I found this water myself.'" He looked me in the eye. "You like that man, Kepler?"

Beard slipped into the shadows on the street. "Best hurry, now," he said over a shoulder, "that fella with the fancy train car is expectin' ya."

Chapter Six

The twitch of a horse's tail was the only movement in the still night. The animal stood tied to a rail in front of the Limping Burro Saloon. I crossed to the platform between the rails and the station building. Moonlight through the window showed the clock behind the station's ticket cage. The long hand touched eleven, the short hand found one.

I jumped down into the train yard. Shadows threatened me. That voice in my head told me that at any moment, a demon in a white gown would dash from the dark and tear at my neck. When a dog barked on some faraway hill, my hand found the pistol in my belt.

I caught hold of the handrail and lifted myself onto the ornate car's landing. I pushed open the door to the vestibule. A musty odor filled the small space. In the shadowy corner, a fresh-killed deer hung. From a knife slash in its throat, drops of blood tapped the bottom of a tin bucket.

I knocked on the door. Warm candlelight spilled out.

A man's deep voice said, "Kepler, I'm so glad you accepted my invitation. Come in. Have a glass of red wine."

No room in Denver's best hotel was furnished as lavishly as that train car. Thick, red carpet cushioned my feet, a rare treat for someone like me, accustomed to dirt streets and wooden boardwalks. Velvet curtains draped the shade-drawn windows.

At the center, on a heavy table, a candelabrum burned and red liquid sparkled in two crystal goblets. My host gestured to a chair and seated himself on one of the couches. Only then did the flicker of the flames allow me to glimpse his face.

"You disappoint me, Kepler," he said. The widow's peak in his hairline reached across his shallow forehead, stopping just above his thick eyebrows. "I know of your inquisitive mind. I thought you'd be full of questions." He plucked a chalice from the table and brought it to his lips. His tongue darted into the blood-red wine. "Please sit."

I bit my tongue to avoid stammering. "The fact that I'm here should speak of my curiosity."

His head leaned back in a laugh. "Well said. Then let me give you the answers before you ask the questions."

Hair the color of coal hung to his massive shoulders. When he peered over the rim of the crystal, I believed his eyes were blue. But as he drank, reflections from the crimson liquid turned them from blue to a deep purple.

"I am called Nicolae Volker. But I intend to be your friend. Call me Nicolae." His dark, hairy hands held the glass near his heart. "You interest me, Kepler. I believe you can be of use to me. And I will make it worth your while."

"Have we met? I'm sure I'd remember."

"I know of your reputation, sir." He raised the cup and his tongue lifted a bit more of the wine into his mouth. "The stories you wrote about Lord Dunraven's hunting expedition amused me. I am completing a similar expedition."

"You know Dunraven?"

"No. We tend to travel in different circles."

"But you're a hunter?"

"I do enjoy the stalk," he smiled. "And, of course, the kill."

I shifted in the chair and reached for the glass of wine but pulled my hand back. In the color, I saw the captain's stained shirt.

"I have acquired land on the pass above town, and I intend to build a retreat for my family. As I will be burdened with other business, I need an overseer to manage the construction, suppliers, and accounts."

"I'm a newspaper reporter." My fingers clumsily rubbed the tabletop near my untouched glass.

Nicolae's face tilted forward and the purple eyes studied me. "I would guess that you're being paid only a few dollars more than the miners in this tired little town. And I'm aware that a bit of poor judgment cost you your last position."

Nicolae set his goblet on the table. He brought both hands together and interlocked his long fingers. "Most likely you have less than five dollars to your name. You took the newspaper job here in Brokeheart out of desperation." One bramble-bush eyebrow arched upward.

"You'd make a good newspaper man. You do your research." My hand found the chalice and I took a mouthful. The wine was sweet but a hint of saltiness swept my mouth.

"It is an acquired taste," he said. "Some never get used to the blend." He paused, then said, "Kepler, I'm prepared to pay you one hundred dollars a week."

"A hundred dollars?" I croaked. A brackish film clung

to my tongue and palate. I took another swallow of wine, but it failed to wash it away.

"Construction will begin within the week. I need you to keep my hirelings from stealing from me."

One hundred dollars. I thought the man toyed with me. My teeth raked the saltiness from my tongue. "What makes you think I wouldn't steal from you?"

He laughed again, softly this time, almost a growl, rolling up from deep in his chest. "Because you're smart enough to realize that opportunities like this come rarely. Doing what I ask will earn you more than larceny. Come, look over the plans for my new home."

In the next instant, Nicolae was on his feet. He padded across the room, pulled open a cabinet and returned with a sheaf of papers. "This is what you will help me build," he said, opening the bundle.

Candles burned to the nub and were replaced with new. Finally, as he slammed the last ledger shut, I was able to meet those strange purple eyes without fear. Though the promise of money lured me, I couldn't keep myself from believing Nicolae was a madman.

He filled my wine glass for the third time. "I've left nothing out. I intend to build my home on the American frontier. And in time, a few invited guests will share all that it will offer. You will write of it, Kepler."

"I can keep a weekly journal of its progress. I'm sure that the papers in Denver—no, from Kansas City to San Francisco—would buy the syndication." The wine made me eager, and words spilled from my mouth almost without my knowing.

"No," a woman's voice called out.

I turned toward the sound. She closed the car's door behind her and stepped from the dimness of the candlelight. The flicker of the light played over skin as white and smooth as mother of pearl. But it was her movements that took my breath. Beneath her pale gown, muscle and sinew stretched and contracted with each step.

"Nothing in the newspapers. We demand privacy, for now," she said. Careful strides brought her to the edge of the table. Her hand found Nicolae's shoulder. "Later, when the time is right, we will want the story shared."

My host's eyes tightened. "I thought you were resting," he said to her. "Did you decide to go out?"

"The moonlight was so inviting. I should have told you." She plucked a twig from her dark hair and let it drop onto the carpet.

I felt her eyes study my face. "I rather like him, Uncle."

I can count on one hand the times I have felt myself blush in the presence of a woman. I leaned away from the table, hoping the shadows would hide the warmth that spread over my cheeks.

"My niece is correct concerning our story's timing." Nicolae leaned back and looked up at the woman. "This creature is Landry. Undoubtedly, word of the construction will spread. The biggest part of your job will be to downplay that news."

Nicolae brushed her hand from his shoulder. "Leave us. You and I will speak later."

Landry did not move. "Have you told him of our customs, Uncle?" She stared with eyes that shared that slight shade of violet.

The muscles in Nicolae's jaws bunched. He reached out and caught the fabric of her dress.

"These customs she speaks of are considered strange by most." His eyes stayed fixed on her, as if I were no longer in the room. "We choose to be reclusive. Some would say to a fault. And I find my most productive hours are late at night. Landry is just now becoming accustomed to these practices. But, Kepler, I am fortunate enough to be able to afford these peculiarities."

He pushed her away.

Landry arched her back. A noise somewhere between a snarl and a sigh came from deep inside of her. "It was my pleasure, Kepler," she said.

She disappeared into the shadows at the back of the room. The swish of her gown brushed on a doorframe and then I heard the click of a lock.

Something in my nature wanted to believe that the woman's entrance was an element of Nicolae's scheme. "Remind me of the money." I tried to hide any skepticism in my voice.

"Kepler," Nicolae raised his voice, "you will be paid the amount we discussed weekly and receive a bonus equal to the sum of your total salary if construction is completed according to schedule."

My mind snapped back to the money. Twenty weeks times one hundred dollars. Then two thousand more. "I'll resign my job at the newspaper." *Why work for pennies when this fortune was waiting?*

"No!" he snapped, his voice harsh at first, then regaining its soothing tone. "It's too soon. I would prefer that you maintain the appearance of your current employment for now. I have every confidence that you can perform both tasks." He stroked his hair. "If we are in agreement, you will pick up your first week's salary at the bank on Monday. With your payment you will receive an envelope with instructions, and each week after that in the same manner."

He held his hand out to mine. The firmness of his grip did not surprise me. "Do we have an agreement?"

I took his hand. "We do." *But*, I told myself, *it's only an agreement as long as the money is in the bank on Monday.*

The silver moon finished its path across the night sky and faded. False dawn sent the first hints of the new day along the eastern mountains.

Monday morning would tell. Would the hundred dollars be at the bank? Or was Nicolae a madman with a grand dream of a palace and empty promises of wealth?

If it were only true, no longer would I be concerned over the next meal, a place to sleep, or the hushed comments of those who thought me a vagabond. More importantly, with the promised cash, I could devote my time to serious writing. In the gray twilight of that Saturday morning, I wondered if my world was about to turn golden.

In the back room of the *Gazette,* I sat back in my chair and thought over the evening's events. The sheriff and others knew of my visit to Nicolae's private train car. Not writing something of the meeting would arouse suspicion. I hurriedly composed two paragraphs about a European hunter on an expedition in the Colorado mountains. I did not mention his name.

I placed the article on the editor's desk along with the story on the miner's wife, stripped off my boots and stretched out on my cot.

My mind pushed the horrors in the alley behind the Months Saloon far away. I forced myself to believe that the vision of the woman hanging in the tree happened a decade ago. I twisted and tossed on the hard bed, anticipating my new fortune. Only as the sun's rays sliced through the window did the day's fatigue win the battle with my excitement.

A dream crept in and found me. I stood in the bottom of a deep hole. When I pushed a shovel into the hard soil, blood flooded into the pit. I clawed at the crumbling dirt, fighting to climb out. As I jerked awake, the last image of my nightmare was Landry smiling down at me.

I lurched from the bed and splashed water from a basin onto my face. My stomach churned and the wine's salty taste came back into my mouth. I stumbled to the door and vomited. Thick red liquid emptied up from my stomach.

Chapter Seven

The coffee in the tin cup burned as hot as the morning sun on my bent neck. I found a spot of shade, plopped down on the rough boardwalk and tried another sip. The brew burned my stomach and brought the vile taste of the wine back to my mouth. I swallowed hard and stared at the ground. A line of ants crossed the dust between the toes of my boots.

Leather harnesses creaked. The undertaker clucked to his team and his buckboard turned from a side street onto Main. Two new pine-board coffins sat in the wagon's bed.

I hoped the captain and Jeff had found peace. I spilled out my coffee on the thirsty dirt, left the cup on the boards and fell in behind the wagon.

At the graveyard, Sheriff Beard stabbed a shovel into new dirt heaped upon the pile I had left next to the grave I dug yesterday. He reached down to the second grave. Father Dowd caught the sheriff's hand and scrambled up. The priest spoke to the sheriff-preacher and Beard shook his head. Then the churchmen walked to the wagon.

Without saying a word, the sheriff and the priest pulled the casket from the buckboard. I found a hold on the end of the coffin. We carried it to the graveside and returned for the other.

"Hurry," the undertaker snapped from his perch on the

wagon seat. “Madison’s payin’, so I gots to get these horses hitched up to the hearse for that miner lady.”

As we tugged the next coffin from the wagon bed, the undertaker popped the end of the reins on the horses’ flanks and trotted his team down off the hill toward his shop.

We lowered each of the pine boxes into the graves. Beard picked up his Bible and opened it. Dry wind snapped at the worn pages. He squinted down at the scripture and was about to speak, when he nodded down the hill. I turned.

May was in the lead and her two girls followed. Their bright-colored dresses had been washed and ironed. May wore a blue feathered bonnet. April carried a scarlet parasol rimmed with tassels. Side by side, the girls from the saloon marched up Graveyard Hill. At the fence, May pinched out her cigar and perched the stub on the top rail of the pickets. Then the three women stepped into the yard and lined up at the end of the open graves.

June cocked her head and stared down at the caskets. The breeze teased at the green ribbon in her white-blond hair. She clutched a lace kerchief.

May looked at the priest, bowed her face a bit and then said, “Read over ’em, sheriff. These’s good men. Had a string a’ bad luck. Both of ’em. We come to say our good-byes.” Her fingers touched an eye. “Let’s get on with it, now. This here’s the first time I’ve locked the front door of my saloon since I bought the place.”

It will not be the sheriff’s soft, halting voice reading the Twenty-Third Psalm, nor the priest’s prayer for the two souls that I will remember. The sounds that will remain in my mind until my own funeral will be the simple music of sandy earth shoveled onto pine wood and three women's voices.

June's innocent soprano sang the first notes. May lifted her chin and words from deep in her tobacco-thickened throat joined in. She elbowed April. The scar-faced black girl hesitated, then warbled the song.

And three whores sang,

Rock of Ages cleft for me,

Let me hide myself in Thee.

After the women left, I tossed the last spade of dirt on the mound over the captain's grave. Beard pushed a wooden cross into the soft dirt and drove it in with the flat of his shovel.

"Thanks, Kepler." His first words since he had read from the Bible.

I could think of no response and only nodded.

He gathered the shovels and tucked the worn Bible under his arm. "Need to check in at the office. I'll be back for the woman's service," he said to Father Dowd and ambled off the hill.

The priest and I stood by the graves. His hands folded together below his bowed head. Then slowly, he made the sign of the cross.

"It was not suicide," Dowd whispered. "Sophia was a young woman full of hope. She looked forward to becoming a mother. She and her husband had plans to build a better life. She would not do such a thing."

I held onto the secret I had seen at the undertaker's: the wounds on Sophia's neck so like the ones on both Jeff and the captain.

"Dead's dead, Father. There's nothing more to do for her."

"You do not believe in something bigger than yourself, Kepler?"

"I know it's your business to teach hope and Heaven. But, no, I have no reason to believe."

"Look around you." He pointed to the blue mountains still capped with the winter's snow. "Does all this not speak of a grand design and a creator?"

"Look, there's hundreds of ways and as many preachers trying to explain. How can you be sure?"

"So there is no hope anywhere?"

"Tell the two we just buried about hope. They died without any." I looked away, tormented by my own words.

One of the undertaker's horses stumbled on the path. The vile man cursed and slapped the reins across its back. The animal tossed its head and snorted, then trudged up the hill. A dozen steps behind the wagon, the crowd of miners and their families followed the black hearse.

"Tell *them* about hope, Father." I spoke from a hurt deep inside me. "Then send them back to their dirt-floored shacks."

Dowd caught my shirt sleeve as I tried to pull away. "Sophia did not kill herself." His eyes pleaded. "She was at the church that evening. So full of life. Find out what happened to her. If not for her family and friends, for yourself." He let loose of my shirt and bowed his head.

I pushed my way through mothers with children's hands tight in their own. Gaunt-eyed old men stepped out of my way. The sad group stopped outside the fence. Father Dowd joined them.

The sounds of muffled sobs and prayers whisked me away from Graveyard Hill. Every blink of my eyes brought Beard's words about the man in the dry well back to me.

I crossed the footbridge over Brokeheart Creek. The trail forked. The priest's church sat up the hill a hundred yards. The other path followed the stream toward town and the miners' shanties. No doubt the way Sophia had tried to find her way home the night she died.

White puffs of down floated from the cottonwoods. They danced on my breath, and with each step I took, spun away in tiny whirlwinds. Tree shade cooled the sweat between my shoulder blades. A gray-brown rabbit plucked at the blades of grass, then scurried away as I walked closer. Wanting to be a schoolboy again, I snatched up a stone to toss at the cottontail. I stopped and peered into the tangle of weeds. Instead of the rabbit, I found Sophia's shoe.

One shoe on. One shoe lost. I had written those very words to describe the image of Sophia's limp body hanging from the tree. I knelt and leaned closer.

In the dust at the trailside, I could see where the toes of a small bare foot had brushed the soil. Two marks along the ground showed where her heel and a shoe-clad foot had been dragged from the soft dirt onto the hard-packed pathway. Down the trail a few more steps, I found the drag marks again.

A half-dozen red-brown drops of dried blood sprinkled through the heat-withered grass.

This place was a half-mile from the tree where we had found her body. I moved along the path, studying the ground. Except for the tracks of what I judged to be a large coyote here and there, I could detect no more signs of blood or drag marks. I looked back. There were no footprints but my own.

Three times I returned to where I had found her shoe.

I re-examined the area. The only evidence was the dried blood and the drag marks.

I left the shoe where it lay. Beard needed to know what I had found. And the priest.

I fought to keep from running to the graveyard and screaming for the sheriff to come and see Sophia's shoe, see the dried blood on the grass, see the marks where someone had dragged her away.

Just in case there might be other evidence, I forced myself to move slowly along the path. I only found animal tracks in the damp soil along the creek bottom until I came to the trampled grass at the tree where we had found Sophia hanging.

I scrambled up the creek bank to the shacks behind Front Street and crossed the alley where the captain and Jeff had bled. I heard shouting. A driver whipped his horses, and his buggy galloped down the street. Men in dirty overalls pushed through the door of a saloon, their work boots clomping away down the boardwalk. I spotted the sheriff. He stood head and shoulders above the crowd gathering near the depot.

A voice from the mob called out, "Where'd ya git 'em?"

A gray-bearded man in a buckskin shirt stood atop the canvas lashed over a loaded freight wagon. He hoisted a dead animal to his shoulders and the limp body hung down to his feet. He held it out for crowd. "Jus' a-ways out of town there." Bright red blood streaked his leather shirt. "Stopped to water my team and seen this ol' devil sneakin' through the oak brush."

He let the carcass drop to his waist. "Took three shots from my Winchester to put 'im down."

From where I stood at the edge of the mob, I could make out the gray fur in his hands.

"Ain't like a wolf to come this close to town," someone said.

The wolf's killer pulled open the animal's jaws. "He's an old one. Look here, how's his teeth's near wore away." Men near the wagon leaned in and nodded. "See these here? I think he tangled with somethin'." He pointed to tears on the wolf's flanks. "Somethin' ran 'im off."

I pushed my way through the crowd, closer to Sheriff Beard.

"Chasin' a she-wolf he couldn't handle, I'll betcha," came from somewhere in the group of men.

"Happens to all of us. Too old to catch a young piece," another responded.

"Good thing the girls at the Months don't run all that fast."

The teamster sprawled the wolf across the canvas. He propped its head on the wagon's wheel. The wolf's dead eyes pinched shut and its tongue lolled from its mouth. Men elbowed closer. Some curled the animal's lips back to gawk at its teeth.

"Poor devil," I heard someone say. "Probably thought there'd be easy pickin's around town here."

"Poor devil, hell. I'll shoot every one I see," the teamster spat. "Wolves'll kill for the pure simple joy of killin'."

Then another voice, "Sheriff, ya think this was what tore up ole Jeff?"

I looked up at Beard's tired face. He let his head nod slightly. "I'd wager on it," he said just loud enough for the crowd to hear.

"Wha' ya goin' do with the hide?" a bald man with a

stained apron tied around his bulging gut shouted from the doorway of a saloon. "I'll give you two dollars for it."

"Throw in three fingers of Redeye and I'll skin it for you," the teamster brayed back.

"Done," the saloonkeeper yelled over the crowd. "Now the rest of ya come in and buy a beer so I can pay this old-timer."

Hands slapped the old man's shirt as he jumped down. Laughter filled the hot air. Little boys crept close with pointed sticks to poke at the dead wolf. Women in bonnets scurried back into the shade.

I caught the sheriff's arm and spun him to face me. He yanked away and stared hard in my eyes.

"Is it that easy?" I said through my teeth. "That wolf is your answer?"

"Kepler, there's things about this town you don't know," he whispered.

"I saw claw marks on Sophia's neck. No wolf hung her in a tree."

"Jeff and the cap'n didn't count for much. Easy answers, settle the folks down. And for the woman–she hung herself. If'n she lived up on the hill, things'd be different." He looked away. "The woman's in the ground. Let her rest."

The cool breeze spread over my face. Gray clouds boiled over the western mountains. The saber point of blue-white lightning sliced the sky. Buildings shuddered in the crack of thunder, and the heavens opened.

People hurried from the open street for the cover of the storefronts. Beard and I stayed anchored where we stood. Every hoof print in the dirt on Front Street filled with water. Wagon wheel ruts flowed like a river. Water dripped from the brim of my hat and soaked my shirt. Beard looked up at the sky. Raindrops coursed through the stubble on his cheeks.

"Needed the rain," he said over the pounding torrents. "It might wash away all this town's sins."

Like it was washing away the tracks and those few drops of Sophia's blood.

Chapter Eight

On a cool September day, Joe Medicine Pony finished brushing down the sorrel. He lifted each of the horse's feet in turn and scraped away the packed mud from the animal's hooves.

A red-bearded man in overalls and railroad stripes leaned on the corral rails next to me. "I heard ya won him in the card game?"

"You heard it wrong," I told him. "Cowhand was holding a jack high straight. He bet his saddle and rig against what I had on the table. I had all the fours. When he was done cussing me, I offered to buy him a train ticket to Denver and give him five dollars for the horse. He cussed some more, then took it."

"Ya been ridin' a lucky streak, Kepler." The railroader wiped his face with a red kerchief. "Took those silver nuggets off my conductor last time we had a layover."

"He told me he won them in a game himself." I watched Joe rub the horse down with handfuls of dry grass. "What can I say, cards been good to me."

"Seems like a lotta things been good to you." He bent and spat a stream of tobacco juice on the fence post. "Yer living in a room at the hotel now. Folks all over the state talkin' about the stories you been writin' about them *poor* miners. But every time we stop in this town, we got a package of fancy new clothes or something' for you. Careful." He spit again. "Lucky streaks tend to play theirselves out."

"Irish, you should know by now, being careful rarely crosses my mind."

He shook his head, then pulled his watch from a pocket in his overalls. "Have Joe load that bald-face fleabag in the train car. We'll be pullin' outta here in a few minutes." Irish pushed away from the fence and marched to the train.

Joe led my white-faced horse to the fence. I took a lump of brown sugar from my pocket, crumbled it into my palm and held out my hand. "Ready for a train ride, Horse?" I stroked the big animal's face. "After we check on the building up there on the mountain, you and me are going to take a hunting trip."

"This good horse," Joe whispered. "Eyes different colors. Mean he sees the spirits." Joe took a pinch of yellow pollen from the leather pouch he wore around his neck and rubbed it down my horse's mane.

I grabbed his wrist. "Tales for children, Joe. No prayer or pinch of medicine dust ever put one dollar in my pocket. I don't believe in spirits. Just good and bad turns of luck."

Joe's dark eyes measured me. He turned and led the horse away.

I gathered my bedroll, saddlebags, and rifle and crossed to the platform. I heard Joe's hand smack the horse's rump and the clomp of hooves on the wooden loading chute.

May's girl, June, smiled at me with eyes as bright as the morning. Her corn silk hair was tied up in ribbons that matched her red dress. "Miss May's sendin' April and me to Denver to pick up some supplies, Kepler. I ain't rode on a train since the one that brought me to Brokeheart." She squirmed on the hard bench. "You don't come down our way no more." Little-girl freckles sprinkled her fresh-scrubbed face. "Not since that bad night." Then she whispered, "I don't take that laudanum no more."

By staying away from Front Street and May's saloon, I kept the horror of those mangled bodies away from my thoughts. The story I had written about the hanged woman, Sophia, had been picked up and published in newspapers across the West. I had become a sort of herald for the plight of oppressed miners. Newspapers asked for further accounts and I obliged. More stories meant more money. Wilson at the *Gazette* enjoyed the new fame. But something deep within me wouldn't let go of the things I had seen that night.

"What's May going to do without the two of you?" I asked, to push the subject away once more.

"Two new girls down der," April said. "Miss May calls one of 'em July. And the other 'un January, 'cause she always comes first," the black girl cackled.

"Boardin'," the conductor called.

April and June snatched up their bundles and stepped onto the train. I followed with my rifle and saddlebags. A peddler in a plaid suit showed his teeth at the girls from his seat at the far end of the car. June sat down in a seat in front of me with her back to the leering man and then picked up a newspaper left by some traveler. She twisted her nose as she stared at the paper. "It says 'Kepler' right here."

I leaned closer and saw my name over a column I had written some weeks before. "It's called syndication. Other newspapers buy my stories. Where's that paper from?"

"Led . . . Leadville," she said.

"Can you read, June?"

"I have trouble with the big words, but I read some. You

write good, Kepler. I told Miss May yer words can make a passel of ma'skeeters sound near romantic."

The locomotive coughed, then sent a whoosh of steam into the crisp air. The whistle shrieked and with a jerk we left Brokeheart.

June leaned out the window. Specks of black cinders bounced on her hair. I knew she took the hand of many a miner, trail hand, or railroader and climbed the stairs of that saloon. Yet some strange innocence clung to her and I would not think of her as the whore she was.

Our train climbed a little basin shaped like a teacup with one side smashed away. The rails followed the curve of the cup, then dropped down onto the saucer, and once more from the saucer to a plain as flat as a table top. In the distance, pine timber darkened the mountain pass the train would climb. Near the top, when the train stopped for water, I would leave, as my habit had become, to check on the progress of Nicolae's lodge.

The source of my lucky streak was not just the cards and my newspaper writings, but the hundred dollars I collected every Monday.

June drifted off to sleep. I took the newspaper from the seat beside her and looked over the front page. The threat of a miners' strike in Leadville seemed imminent. The workers were rumored to seek three dollars a day. They cited poor conditions in the mine and inability to support their families.

Just below the fold, an inky picture taken at the rail-yard covered the page. Publisher Wilson was in negotiations to add new presses that would produce the pictures for his paper in Brokeheart, so I studied this closely. There was the usual shadowing, but this illustration was particularly clear.

The tip of my finger touched the images of the building, railcars, and locomotive. Even the features of the people were discernible. One of those faces alarmingly so.

The woman's dark hair drew me at first. But even in the depiction on the page, her animal grace was apparent. And from the grays and blacks, my mind wanted to see that hint of purple in her eyes. Landry was in Leadville. Nicolae would be with her.

I tucked the paper into my saddlebags.

The train eased to a stop at the top of the pass. I signed for a bunk of lumber. Workers at Nicolae's lodge offloaded the wood and other supplies from a flatcar. The big Irishman hollered for his brakemen to fill the boiler from the water tower and then walked the length of his train.

"I always check the brakes 'fore 'en we start down to Denver," he said, leaning between the cars to check the wheels.

"It's steeper than a cow's face and twisty as a hot rattler all the way down."

I walked with him to the car where my horse waited. Irish slid back the side door and we pulled down the ramp. The big sorrel snorted as I climbed in. I caught hold of his halter and untied him.

The animal lifted his head as he stepped from the shadows of the car and his nostrils' flared, pulling in fresh air. He blew his lungs empty and tossed his head when his hooves touched the ground.

June and the other passengers milled around, waiting to board for the next leg of the trip to Denver.

"He's purty," June called to me. "What do you call him?"

"The waddie I got him from just called him Horse. He said he didn't want to hang a name on something he might have to eat."

June's hands covered her mouth and laughter poured through her fingers. She came closer and reached up, stroking the horse's flanks. June tangled her fingers in his coarse mane. "Give him a pretty name, Kepler. You know all those words."

"Ol' Joe said horses with a blue eye and a brown one can see the spirits. Shall I call him Seer?"

"It's a fittin' name." June's cheek touched Seer's withers and she held her face there.

I toed a stirrup and tossed my leg over the saddle. Seer and I fell in behind the lumber wagon. In half an hour the trail left the creek side and climbed through a stand of dark timber.

In the shadows of the twisted pines, I pulled my jacket tight across my chest. The sounds of the birds faded as we climbed. Horse hooves on stone and wagon creaks were the only noises. My hand found the butt of my rifle in its holster just to be sure it was there.

Another hour and the wagon trail led us down a north-facing slope to a small lake. Seer measured each step down the rocky trail. Dark green moss circled the rough gray trunks of trees as big around as wagon wheels. Sharp sounds from hammers and chisels shaping granite into blocks drifted to us. Seer tossed his head. A circle of white showed around his blue eye. He balked, then crow-hopped toward the edge of the trail. His whinny cut through the air and the noise of the hammers stopped.

"Beautiful horse, Mister Kepler." A small Greek man strode down from the building site.

I swung down from the saddle and tied Seer tightly to a tree.

"Rosie, you've made considerable progress since my last visit."

Two-story stone walls were in place. Three men hung from a makeshift scaffold slinging mortar into gaps of the blocky chimney at the center of the house. Another team of workers hoisted great timber beams onto the roofline.

"My men good workers," he said. "They know winter coming and they want to get home to their families."

"There's a keg of beer from Denver and real beef steaks with the supplies. Tell them that Nicolae is pleased with the reports I send him. And there's a bottle of Kentucky whiskey for you, my friend. Show me what you've accomplished and then we'll have a drink together."

Chapter Nine

Rosie's brown finger traced the crumpled plans I had first seen in Nicolae's train car. "With the lumber you brought us today, we lay the upstairs floor. God willing, the roof will be complete before week's end." He picked up a glass and sighed before sipping the amber liquor.

"Window glass will be here in two weeks." I said. "And . . ."

Rosie twirled his glass in the gold lantern light that filled the tent.

"And Nicolae will be here the week after. He wants to see for himself." I looked Rosie in the eye. "We're six weeks from his deadline."

"He's a harsh man."

"You're being paid well. Your men, too. He's given you anything you asked for."

Rosie finished his whiskey in a single gulp. "Kepler, my men, they don't like him. And the woman," he lowered his voice. "She has the eyes of an animal. They say she evil."

"You have a big bonus coming if you can be finished in six weeks." *And a bigger one for me*, I thought.

"I know, I know." He looked out of the tent into the black night. "When Nicolae was here last . . ." His voice trailed away and he reached for the bottle.

"What is it?"

"H-he did not tell us he was coming. When we go to the train to get supplies, his train car is on the siding."

Rosie would not look at me.

"He and the woman come with the wagon. First blocks of the walls are in place. I show him, and we study these plans together." Whiskey spilled over the rim of his glass as he lifted it to his mouth.

"I tell the cook to make nice meal. Nicolae and his lady, they come to this big tent and do not eat with us. Strange, I think. But no matter."

Rosie's shoulders slumped. He held the glass in both hands and rested it on his legs.

"That night, I tell the men to picket the mules in the meadow by the lake so they could graze in the moonlight. We all go to bed."

His eyes studied the glass in his hands.

"It was late. Maybe two in the morning. The mules, they make big noise. I think maybe bear. Maybe mountain lion. A group of us run down there with lanterns. Torches."

"So what has this to do with–"

Rosie raised his hand. "Have you ever heard a mule scream with pain, Mister Kepler?"

The lantern on the table beside him hissed and grew dim, starving for fuel. Rosie's damp eyes looked at me.

"No other sound like it. In the shadows from the torches I see the mule thrash on the ground, legs kicking. Something is running away. One man has rifle and fires a shot. I hear woman scream. Then all is quiet."

I leaned closer. "They tell me a mountain lion can sound like a woman's scream."

"The mule is dead." He stretched his neck back and

his hand touched his throat. "Its neck is broken. And much blood. We look for tracks. Find nothing."

"Rosie, what does any of this have to do—" He cut me short.

"I go to tent to tell Nicolae. Tent is empty." He reached for the whiskey and filled his glass. He held the bottle up for me. I shook my head. "Next morning, two of my men are gone, too."

"Nicolae and Landry went back to their train car, that's all. Your men got spooked. Lit out for home."

"No. I send letters to their families. They are not home."

"They could be anywhere. There're dozens of mines hiring men all the time."

"Tell Nicolae not to come," his voice pleaded.

"I can't do that. This is his—"

"Did you know about his last visit?"

"No. But he doesn't need to tell me." I shook my head. "Rosie, all this about the mule and the two men you can't find means nothing. Your job is to build this house. And to get it done before the snow flies. Six more weeks 'til deadline. Think of the money you'll have."

"But I have no control when the snows come. God willing, we'll be ready."

"If I were you, I'd be sure your men forget this foolishness and work hard," I told him. "Don't count on God." *You silly old man,* I thought.

Without another word, the tired builder left the tent. I blew out the lantern, stretched out on the makeshift cot and prayed sleep would come. But images of dead men with their throats ripped away kept me company. And I imagined the cries of a dying mule and the screams of a woman.

From my bed, I could hear Seer pace the pole corral just yards from my tent. I heard him snort when the night breezes stirred the trees.

I tossed and turned. Finally I sat up, wrapped the blankets over my shoulders and groped in my saddlebags for a match and candle. From its dim light, I found my last letter from Nicolae. I held the paper close to the flame and squinted at the postmark on the envelope. My fingers clawed deep into the pouch for the newspaper June had found on the train. Holding it to the light, I saw the paper was dated the same day as Nicolae's letter.

For several minutes, my mind played with this new tangle. But when my eyes fell on that newspaper again, the blanket on my shoulders could not hold back the chill that rose up deep within me.

At the bottom corner of the front page, above an advertisement for the local pharmacy, four words were printed in bold letters: "Body Found in Alley." In the shimmer of the candle, I read the few words.

> *The body of a known vagrant was found by a storekeeper early Tuesday morning. The cause of death could not be discerned, as it appeared wild animals had despoiled the body.*

Sickness tore at my stomach. I pulled back the tent flap and gasped for the cool air.

The first gray of dawn climbed the ridge above the half-finished building. The roof timbers cast shadows like the ribs on some discarded carcass.

Right then, I made up my mind to go to Leadville. I would tell Wilson that I wanted to do research for an article on the pending miner's strike. Many things confused me, but I was certain of one. The events in Brokeheart, the missing workers, and this new death in Leadville had all happened when Nicolae had been near.

And the woman, Sophia? Those drops of dried blood and drag marks I had found that day before the rain? Could they be a part of this, also?

I knelt by the lake, dipped my kerchief into the ice-cold water and wiped my face and neck. Morning sun sent a hundred rainbow patterns off the meadow grass, stiff with frost. It would have been a peaceful scene, except that I knew this was the meadow where something had snapped the mule's neck and stained these grasses with the animal's blood. I let Seer drink his fill and then swung into the saddle.

Rosie's workers left the cook tent as I rode by. They gathered tools. Near the building, I heard the first hammer strike the granite. Rosie came out and looked up at me.

"I'm heading back to Brokeheart. Rosie, I decided last night that I'll be here for Nicolae's visit. Believe me, you're doing a good job and my report will say that. Anything else you need?"

Rosie clamped a cigarette in his lips and shook his head.

"On Nicolae's maps I saw a way out of this valley that might save some time. Do you know of it?"

Smoke filtered from his nose. "There's an old prospector's trail just wide enough for a horse that climbs the hillside through the trees. Very steep. At the top of mountain, you follow Severed Finger Creek to next valley. It will save you several hours." He looked up to where his men began their day's work. "I gave my word I will finish this. My word is good. Go with God, Mister Kepler. I will see you in few weeks," he said and walked away.

I found the trail, and Seer followed its switchbacks up the canyon face. He no longer fought my hands on the reins as he had when we entered this valley.

We left the shadowy timber near the ridge top. The sound of the tools and men's voices had faded away. Pale aspens, bright with fall colors, crowded the slope.

Seer's ears picked up the sound of the running water before mine. I stroked his neck and let the sun drive away the chill of the sleepless night. We skirted a gray boulder as big as a boxcar and followed a worn strip of dirt through the grass. The sound of the creek grew louder and Seer quickened his pace, eager for the water.

With a jerk, the horse flung his head back. He shied to the side of the trail and lurched into a hard turn. I yanked back the reins and grabbed for the saddle horn, but it was too late. I pitched from the saddle onto the gravel, grinding my gloves into the grit.

"Cussed horse," I said, half under my breath. I caught hold of the reins as I scrambled to my feet. Seer pulled the latigo tight and backed away. He tossed his head and fought me, nostrils flaring and eyes pulled wide. I snatched up my hat and jerked Seer. The animal sat back and refused to move.

It was as if the horse had sensed their spirits. In the next second, I found Rosie's missing men.

Weeks on the mountainside had done their work. Skin as dry as worn leather stretched taunt over bone and ribs. The first was on his back. Ropes of dried entrails fell from his torn stomach. The man's chin tucked against his shoulder, brown blood staining what was left of his shirt. No more than three steps away lay the second body. His head lay at an odd angle, connected to the body by no more than a flap of skin. His pants were ripped away. Something had feasted on the meat of his buttocks and legs.

I dropped onto my heels and stared into the dirt, wishing all this away. Seer tugged on the reins. I refused to look again. I led Seer back up the trail and tied him to a tree.

Forcing myself back to the clearing, I knelt by the bodies and studied the carnage. A gold wedding band on a withered finger caught the sunlight. Tears flooded my eyes and I cried for his family.

Now, I had seen dead animals before. I knew what time and weather could do to a carcass. Scavengers and insects creep in to tear and carry away. A bear or big cat will hide their kill until they come back for a next meal.

These men bore none of those signs. It was as if, after their last terrible minutes of life, their bodies had sprawled here waiting for their spirits to call out to Seer. Not a predator's track, not a single bug disturbed the gruesome scene.

"Wolves'll kill for the pure, simple joy of killing," the teamster had said that day in the street. But would they drag their kill two miles up a mountain?

Now I held two secrets: Sophia's lost shoe and these bodies on the mountain. But if I told, who would believe me?

With a tin plate from my saddlebags, I scraped a shallow grave in the hard mountain dirt. I pulled the ring from the one man's shriveled finger; then, as gently as I could, I eased the two bodies into the hole. The mid-day sun shone down from its peak in the sky as I covered the mound with rocks.

I made camp where the creek left the mountain and

nursed a fire all night long. Though the blaze burned at my face, night's cold draped across my back. Night noises played in the trees. I levered a cartridge into the breach of my Sharps rifle and stared into the darkness until morning.

Chapter Ten

Just after nightfall the next day, Seer and I rode into Brokeheart. We dodged the horses and wagons crowded along Front Street. Coal-oil lamps flickered in a dozen windows. I could hear music from the Months Saloon. I left Seer and my gear at the livery and followed the piano notes toward town. Grave dirt still clung to my shirt.

Sheriff Beard stepped up on the boardwalk beside me. "Thought ya was gonna spend some time in the hills and come back with fresh venison, Kepler," he said. "Ya look plumb wore out. Somethin' happen out there?"

"No." I looked up at the one man in Brokeheart who had become my friend. I didn't want to lie to him but couldn't put into words the things I had seen. "Couldn't find any sign of game. Thought it was best that I just come on in."

"This good weather we been havin' might be keepin' the elk up high yet. Where ya headed now?"

"I need a drink." I wiped my face on my sleeve. "Then a bath and good night's sleep. I'm thinking on going to Leadville tomorrow."

"You take more baths then anyone in this here town, Kepler." His eyes narrowed. "Watch yourself, hear me? The railroad's got a crew in town tonight. Took the guns off'n a buncha cowhands. Top it off, Madison and some of his are prowlin' Front Street. He don't hold you in too high a regard after what ya wrote in the paper 'bout how he treats his miners. Just maybe you oughta head over to the Chinaman's and get cleaned up, have a drink at the hotel and go up to your fancy room."

"Thanks for the advice, but I need that drink first. Maybe two."

Beard looked down at me. "You packin' that hideout pistol on your hip?"

"No," I lied for the second time.

"Look, my hands are full tonight with all the goin's on. I don't want to have pull your butt out of the fire. So take care."

'Numb' was the only word to describe me. My muscles were numb from digging a grave and two days on horseback. My mind was numb from trying to piece together what I thought I knew about Sophia, the two dead drunks, and Rosie's men on the mountain. Nicolae and Landry somehow played into this. *How* was one question. But *why* was an even a bigger one. Why would a man with Nicolae's money and means have any part in those deaths?

If what the sheriff had just told me about Madison prowling tonight was right, I decided that the whiskey at the Months Saloon would be the best remedy for my tired body. I didn't see a mine superintendent like Madison lowering himself to visit May's place. There was better whiskey at a half a dozen places on Front and higher-class girls to scratch that kind of itch. The more I thought, the more I was sure that May's whiskey would be the best tonic for saddle sores. It might do something for my tired head, also.

I pushed around a mud-splattered horse tied to a hitching post on the street's edge. The door to the Months stood wide open, as always. The old man who plunked on the piano managed to miss the broken keys, but I didn't recognize the tune he was playing.

The railroad crew had picked May's. Those who weren't at the tables leaned two deep on the bar. I spotted the beat-up hats of two drovers at the poker table. One pitched his cards on the tabletop, hooted, and raked a pile of chips toward his side of the boards. A man dressed in conductor blues dropped his head into his hands. He came up for air and downed a shot of whiskey. The fourth man at the table shook his head. Even in the shadows, he looked familiar. I had guessed wrong about Madison.

April stood behind the bar, her scar livid in the lamplight. She cackled and slung mugs of beer to the railroad hands. When she turned for a bottle of whiskey, one man grabbed for a handful of her skirts.

May stepped up from behind him and pinned his forearm to the bar with the wooden mallet she used to tap the kegs. "Even a touch will cost you, sonny," she hollered, then blew a cloud of her cigar smoke in the man's face.

The piano player banged harder, but laughter from two dozen working men drowned out his melody.

I slipped into the spot the red-faced man surrendered. May found her way around the bar and sloshed whiskey into the glass she put in front of me.

"Good to have ya back, stranger." She pinched out the cigar stub and perched a flabby arm on the bar planks. She nodded toward the picture of the naked woman over the bar. "First 'un's on her. The second'll cost ya double."

I dug a silver dollar out my vest and laid it on the bar. May covered the coin with her hand and snatched it away.

"Let me know when that runs out," I said.

"Girls said they seen ya on the train a couple days back, otherwise, I'da thought ya was dead, Kepler."

"I've been busy."

"Too busy to stop fer a drink?"

I held my empty glass out. May splashed it full.

"That young'un, June, reads me everything you write in the *Gazette*. You're makin' quite a name for yourself. And some enemies, I reckon. You might want to finish that drink and get on outta here 'fore Mister Madison sees ya. He's losing at cards tonight and 'll be looking for any excuse to make trouble."

"I thought Madison played cards up the street." The whiskey warmed my empty stomach. I glanced back at the card game. Madison pounded a fist on the table. The cowboy whooped and reached for the table's pot.

"Since ya been writin' 'bout his mine, he feels a mite more comfortable here. Respectful folks are lookin' down their noses at him." She tipped her head at the corner behind the poker table. "And he keeps them two goons he hired right close."

Whiskey has always brought me courage, even in the times courage wasn't what I needed. Fatigue from the trail ride coaxed me to take her advice. But something wouldn't let me listen.

I eyed the two men leaning on the wall in the shadowy corner behind Madison's chair. One wore a bowler hat. He fidgeted like a scared rodent and picked at his fingernails. The other was nearly as tall as I am. I guessed he outweighed me by fifty pounds. The power was in his chest and shoulders. As he rolled a cigarette, his eyes never left the room.

"I'd like to hear how June's trip to Denver went. She

seemed excited." I turned my back to May and leaned on the edge of the bar.

"Upstairs."

I jerked my head around and looked at her. "With a . . ."

"No," she said. "I sent her up to rest. Last I knew she was sittin' on the roof a-singin' to that cat of hers. June's still too young and timid for a rowdy crowd like this 'un. Finish your drink and git on outta here."

"I gave you a dollar. I might want to stay 'til it's gone."

She snatched the bottle from beside me. "The price of whiskey just went up. Don't want no trouble in my place, Kepler."

The little man in the round hat touched Madison on the shoulder. Madison pushed the hand away and slapped his cards on the table. The little man's face tightened, showing sharp teeth, and he pointed at me. Madison pushed back his chair and stood up. He said something over his shoulder. The big man exhaled a cloud of smoke and then walked toward the front door.

The men on either side of me stepped away. I caught the corner of my jacket and tucked it behind my right hip. Making sure my hands were in plain sight, I moved the whiskey glass to my left hand. My right stroked my chin.

The piano went silent. Three men pushed their way out the front door around Madison's big friend. Floorboards creaked under Madison's boots. I thought I knew what quiet sounded like. On the mountain, digging that grave, the sound of my own breathing was the only noise. Now it was as if no one in the bar breathed. The thump of my heart banged like an axe on green wood. I moved my fingers from my chin to the front of my shirt.

Then a cat yowled.

June slipped in the front door. Her satiny red dress caught the glimmer of lantern light. Mr. Buggs, her big yellow cat, was folded in her arms.

Madison's voice rumbled. "Judas Priest, May. I've been sittin' at that table just givin' my money to that cowboy. Might as well put what little I have left to good use." His eyes never left mine. "I'm goin' to treat my boys."

Madison nodded at the big man blocking the front door. "Hayden there, and Oscar." The rat-faced man licked his lips. "Want to take this little lady upstairs. How much is that gonna cost me?"

The cat flopped out of June's arms, then darted around the bar for the backroom. June's hands never dropped from her breasts. Her fingers tangled in the sleeves of her dress and squeezed until her knuckles turned white. "No," she whispered.

Anger boiled up until its flames licked my face. My fingertips touched my belt, edging closer to my hidden pistol. Hayden moved to the center of the room, just to my right.

"You're a mite late, Madison." May's voice was calm. "Kepler jus' give this here silver dollar to spend the night with the girl," she said, holding up the coin. "Ain't that right, Kepler?"

My tongue stuck to the roof of my mouth. I wanted to curse Madison, but I only nodded. June crossed the room. She looked down at the floor until she passed Madison then went to the stairs.

Madison worked his jaw muscles. Oscar stepped from behind him and I saw the glint of gunmetal under his coat.

I sensed May move behind me. Her elbows bumped the bar and a gun's hammer clicked.

"Madison, this here is a cut-down eight gauge," May

said. I saw the muzzles of her shotgun out of the corner of my eye.

May bit down on her cigar and continued. "It don't need aimin'. You just sorta point it at trouble and touch it off. If'n I have to use it, I'm goin' to send a bill to that mine of yours. The cost to clean you off'n the wall behind you. Kepler, go with June," she said.

"We're leavin', May." Madison signaled to his men. Oscar adjusted his hat with both hands. Then he called to me, "Kepler, you might need to plug your nose. There's horse sweat and cow flop from a dozen ranch hands on that bed."

June climbed to the second stair step. I was behind her. I wanted to pull my pistol but my fingers reached out and stroked the satin dress at the small of her back. Through the fabric, June trembled. Without moving my hand, I followed her up the stairs.

I glanced back from the landing. May's scattergun still lay on the bar. Every eye watched June turn the knob to her room. The piano began to play "Clementine".

June lifted the glass on a lamp next to her bed. She struck a match and touched the wick. The light licked at the gray shadows and played over the bedcovers. A basin and pitcher stood on a chest of drawers. June's hairbrush and mirror lay next to the lamp. She never turned to look at me.

Newspaper pages tacked to the wall rustled in the breeze from the window. I moved closer, and in the dim light I saw my name on the stories she had saved.

When I turned, her back was still to me. She brushed her hair away and unbuttoned the collar of her dress. The cloth slipped from her shoulders. A splash of freckles, like the ones on her nose, speckled her smooth skin.

"June," I felt my own voice tremble. "You said you could read, but you had trouble with some of the big words." I tore one of the pages from the wall. "Show me which ones and I'll try to teach you."

I stepped closer, caught the dress's neckline and pulled it back up. My rough fingers grazed her soft, cool skin.

Chapter Eleven

Sunbeams as golden as June's cat melted away the shadows. Mr. Buggs curled up on the bed next to her. The rhythm of June's steady breathing was the only interruption to the peaceful morning. I stood up from the straight-back chair where I had dozed through the night, opened the door and left.

May would look after June. I was sure of that. Whatever Madison had sought to prove last night had been aimed at me and not the girl. A time would come when I'd have to face him. But for now, I wanted to find out more about the body in Leadville. And Nicolae.

I stopped at my hotel room long enough to get clean shirts. From an envelope hidden beneath one of the drawers in the writing desk I filled my money belt with a hundred dollars in paper bills, then dumped a box of pistol cartridges into my jacket pocket.

Burros brayed in the mine's corrals. Somewhere near the train station a rooster crowed and the town began to wake up.

Joe Medicine Pony and Hogan, the old man who brought the dead wolf into town, each led a team of horses from the stable.

"Had quite a night, huh, Kepler?" the teamster said. "Heard May showed Madison and his boys the ornery end of her shotgun jus' so ya could spend the night pickin' ticks off'n that tow-headed whore."

Most likely the man could neither read nor write, but he plainly saw the message on my face.

"Didn't mean nothin' by it," he said sheepishly. "If'n I was you I'd steer clear of them two that Madison put on the payroll. The big fella's hell for stout. Heard he busted a man's back in a bar fight over in Fairplay. But it's the other'n, I'd be watchin'." He spat on the ground between the horses' legs. "That Oscar claims he's a *pistolero*. Wears a big Colt pistol and ties it down all snug-like. Folks say he keeps a derringer in his belt and even sleeps with it. Other day, he shot a miner's kid's dog just fer barkin'."

I led Seer from his stall in the stable and tied him to the corral. When I returned with my saddle and gear, the old man and the Indian were harnessing their teams.

"Where ya headed?" Hogan asked.

"I have business in Leadville."

"You're welcome to ride along with us if'n you choose." He tilted his head down the street.

At the other end of Front Street, Hayden and Oscar sat on their own horses. They watched my every move. Even at that distance, I saw the little man's tongue lick his jagged teeth.

"All by your lonesome, you'd be askin' for trouble. Men like that ain't likely to mess with the three of us. Tie your horse to the back of Joe's wagon and jump on up with him. He don't talk near as much as me." Hogan pulled the rifle he had used to kill the wolf from his wagon and levered a shell into the Winchester's chamber.

It's uphill all the way to Leadville. A man on horseback would make better time than wagons with teams of four. Every half mile the road turned back hard on itself to climb the mountain. At every switchback, a man alone would be easy prey for a hired gun's carbine.

Smoke from Hogan's corncob pipe drifted back through the smell of pine. No clouds marred the blue sky. I wanted it to be peaceful, but I kept my thumb curled around the hammer of the Sharps in case violence came.

I had only heard Joe cluck to his horses. It was past noon and neither one of us had spoken. The teamster bellowed a bawdy song and cursed his team.

"How much further, Joe?"

"Night find us before we find town."

I clutched the big rifle tighter.

"Road," Joe said without taking his eyes from the horses, "it make straight. Soon few trees. Hard for men to get close."

"You think they're following us?"

He nodded. "We stop for water." He took one hand from the reins and touched his nose. "I smell their tobacco."

"You sure? He's been puffing on the pipe all day." I gestured toward the wagon in front of us.

"Make different smoke."

"You're sure?"

Joe nodded.

I twisted around on the hard seat and looked at the road behind us. "So it's true all I've heard about Indians. You see better, hear better, and smell better than whites."

"No. Indian need things to live. White man no need. Live in city. Put wolf in cage, he forgets how to do things. Wolf in forest no forget."

The horses strained in their harness. Joe chanted a few words I didn't understand and the wagon made the steep turn around the switchback.

"Joe, remember that first day we met? You walked me up Graveyard Hill? But wouldn't go into the cemetery?"

"I remember."

"You told me that the town was evil."

"I see the way trees move in wind. Birds' songs different. Man die."

"You saying that when that man I dug the grave for died, nature changed?"

"Man in train car change harmony."

I thought carefully about what his few words tried to tell me. The man in the train had to be Nicolae. My own investigations placed Nicolae in the proximity of other deaths.

"So by just being in town, the man changed some balance in nature?"

"Man come. His spirit make him kill."

Joe tugged at the leather thong that held the pouch he kept in the front of his shirt. He pulled the leather bag open with his teeth and with one hand free from the reins, took a pinch of the yellow pollen and flicked it into the mountain breeze.

"No more words," he said. He pushed the small bag into his shirtfront and chanted to the horses.

Indian superstitions, I told myself. No explanation for the deaths. The sheriff had been right. A drunk staggers into the alley, falls and hits his head. An old wolf, too feeble to hunt for itself, finds an easy meal. The wolf comes back the next night a little bolder and finds the captain. Maybe.

If it happened it Brokeheart, then why not something similar in Leadville?

I heard a branch snap.

The teamster hollered out, "Whoa." Joe eased our wagon to a stop.

A cascade of dirt and stones slid from the steep roadside. The debris bounced off the wagon wheel under the seat where I sat. The Sharps was on my shoulder before my mind wished it there. I thumbed the hammer back and my finger found the trigger. Joe touched my side. Just then a doe and her fawn skittered off the hillside. They stopped short of the wagons and then bolted down the hill away from us.

Joe's chant sounded like a prayer of thanks. He raised his hand. "Harmony," he said to me.

We saw the lights of Leadville two hours before our wagons' wheels rolled onto its streets. We heard the noise of those streets sooner still.

This was a city was in motion. Wagons of every description crowded the streets. Mules and burros brayed. A thousand voices sounded. And a thousand more answered those.

Lamplight shined from every window. Hawkers called from barroom doors. Workmen with mine dust on their clothes pushed by dandies dressed in black. Cowboys, teamsters, and riffraff joined the parade.

At the barns, the teamster and Joe unharnessed their worn teams.

Hogan told me, "There's stables on Third that'll keep your horse. You'll pay dearly for a stall, but they're good people and you'll have no worries. Find a big white house on Fifth, tell the widow woman you rode in with me and she'll give you a room and board. The Indian and me'll sleep here with the wagons."

I found two silver dollars in my pocket. "Buy your dinner on me."

"Obliged." He took the coins. "Kepler, stash the rifle. But keep that pistol of yours handy-like. Madison's boys could be anywhere. They ain't likely to cause trouble on the streets. But keep your nose to the wind and an eye on the shadows."

I stabled Seer in a stall that cost more than the lodgings I secured for myself. After putting my gear in the room, I set off for the railyards. In the morning, I planned to introduce myself at the newspaper office and see what more I could learn about the body found in the alley. But for now, I needed to be sure Nicolae was still in town.

Women in their finest and men in dark suits huddled in the chill as they left the night's performance at Tabor's Opera House. I fell in behind a group of eight young men who sauntered down Harrison Avenue. The leader of this gaggle, a light-haired dandy, swept off his silk hat and fumbled with his cape. The perfume he had daubed into his long hair left a sweet trail in the dusty night air. He eyed my dirty trail clothes and snickered to one of his friends as I passed them.

The clank of boxcars led me from the saloon-lined street to the train station. Unlike Brokeheart, the activity of loading and unloading didn't end at sundown. Flames from a bonfire leaped higher than a man's head and cast a shadowy ring around the yard. Men paused near the fire, holding their hands out to its glow, before returning to their work. I skirted the ring of light and searched the dark tracks for Nicolae's private car.

It was not in the shadows where I had expected to find it. The car sat near the depot building. Light from the candelabrum I remembered so well painted each of the windows and spilled from the open door. I heard the sounds of laughter as shadows passed by the windowpanes.

A carriage pulled to a stop close to the station. Two men and two women climbed down. One of the men waved a hand to the driver and the wagon drove away. The two couples made their way to Nicolae's train car.

I heard voices behind me. I eased the handgun from my belt and pressed my back tight against the side of the building where I stood. The long-haired dandy I had seen minutes before was a full stride ahead of his pack of followers. He ran the last few steps, caught hold of the handrail and lifted himself onto the platform at the back of the car. Landry stepped into the pale light. The young man caught her in his arms and lifted her from her feet.

Five quick steps took me from the corner of the building to the bonfire. I knelt down, pulled the brim of my hat over my face and held my hands out to the warmth. Through the blaze I watched Nicolae join the group. As he emerged from his train car, he lifted a crystal goblet. The liquid in the glass glowed crimson.

Just then, from a church steeple, a bell tolled. Nicolae, Landry, and their group went silent and then with one voice they began to count each strike of the bell.

"Nine . . . ten," they chanted. "Eleven . . . twelve."

An eerie chill stole down my spine.

Nicolae pulled the door to his car shut. The group

marched across the railyards toward town. While the others held their winter wraps tight against the night chill, Nicolae and Landry wore no coats.

Though what happened next seemed small at the time, it is the image I retain when I think of that cold night. A cur dog trotted from the shadows. It held its ground as the group came toward it. The animal snarled. Landry, still on the arm of her tall man, turned her face toward the dog and made a shrill barking noise. The dog yelped and ran into the darkness with its tail tucked between its legs. When those around Landry laughed at the frightened animal, Nicolae's voice sounded the loudest.

I darted to the shadows along the buildings. Careful to stay a block behind, I followed Nicolae's assembly toward Harrison Avenue. In front of the Delaware Hotel, they met several more people. Nicolae shook hands with the men and then led both groups up the side stairs of the hotel building.

Landry, still on the arm of her beau, was the last. She pushed her friend inside and stood on the landing. Her head tilted back and her breasts heaved as she drank in a deep breath. In the soft light, I saw the purple tint of her eyes in the grays and blacks of the shadows all around her. The muted sound of violins floated above the street. Light shimmered around the closed hotel room curtains. Landry took a last look at the moon and the door shut behind her.

Oscar's bowler hat made my decision about what to do next for me. The little man staggered out the door of the Golden Burro Saloon next to his giant companion. Oscar's hand hung above the Colt revolver in his holster. He tripped and bumped into Hayden. The big man lit a cigarette, and then the two pushed their way into the next barroom.

With Madison's men prowling the streets, I knew it would be best to return to my room.

The clerk pinned the register book to the hotel desk with the stump of his severed arm. He squinted at the morning sun through the front window, then dipped a quill in the inkwell and made an "X" on the map he had drawn for me. "The newspaper building is right there. You can't really miss it."

I brushed the melting snow from the shoulders of my mail-order coat. "Thank you, sir." I turned to look over the lobby of the Delaware Hotel. "Where would you suggest a hungry man could find a good breakfast?"

"The food in the hotel's dining room is excellent. They bring me a plate each morning. It's pricey, but judging by the cut of your clothes, you can afford it." He tugged at his string tie and smiled.

"You wouldn't just be saying that because you work here, would you?"

He raised the damaged arm. "After my accident at the mine, the hotel was good enough to give me a job here. I do everything I can to repay the favor. But I'm sure you'll find the food to your liking."

"Thank you, Mister . . . ?"

"Collier. Jefferson Collier."

"One more thing, Mr. Collier. I've heard that this hotel hosts some sort of late-night parties. After the opera?"

Collier eyes dropped to the desktop. "I know of no such events, sir."

"It must be a different hotel here on Harrison."

"Perhaps." He didn't look up.

"Oh, and Collier," I leaned forward on the desk. "If my current accommodations don't work out, would you have a room available here?"

"I'm sorry, sir. All of our rooms are booked for the remainder of the month."

I insisted on a table in the dining room where I could watch the activity on Harrison. The waiter showed me to a table near the doors. Snowflakes the size of silver dollars drifted down from the steel-gray sky. Silvery vapor trailed from the mouths and noses of those who walked by. I ordered breakfast and asked the waiter to bring me a copy of the morning newspaper.

It was my first full meal since the Greek stew I had shared with Rosie and the workers at Nicolae's lodge. I savored the eggs and sausage as I unfolded the paper and scanned the front page.

Collier's face appeared at the door to the dining room. He raised his good hand to shield his mouth and spoke to a man behind him.

I lifted the paper and pretended to read. Long curls, wet with the snow, clung to the tall man's face. The scent of his cologne drifted across the room. He peered around the doorframe for an instant and then was gone.

It was the man who had held Landry in his arms last night.

The office of the *Leadville Herald Democrat* sat a block off Harrison. The woman behind a long counter took my business card without looking up. I watched her read the card. Suddenly her head jerked up and she studied me for a moment. I smiled. Then she hurried to a side office.

Even above the noise of the presses, I heard the scramble of hard shoes on the wood floors. A man came out the door slipping his arms into his suit coat. The short mustache on his upper lip quivered and he reached out to shake my hand.

"Kepler, it's my pleasure." He pumped my arm. "Sam Thomas, here, managing editor. Old man Wilson let you out of Brokeheart?"

"I wanted to spend a few days here to learn what I can about the pending strike at the mines. Thought it best if I stop in and introduce myself."

"I was hoping you'd tired of that little town and were looking for a position here." Thomas raised his eyebrows. "You've made quite a name for yourself. I think we've run most everything you've written."

"I'm flattered, sir. I'm happy in Brokeheart for now, but that doesn't mean sometime in the future . . ."

"When you're ready, let me know. And we'll do anything we can to help while you're here. Come into my office and we'll talk."

Thomas motioned me around the counter and into his office. He shut the door and settled into his chair. "Cigar?" He opened a box and held it out to me.

I shook my head. He took one from the box, bit off the end and tucked the cigar in the corner of his mouth without lighting it.

"You know that my writing about the conditions at the mines has earned me some . . . How should I say this? Well, not everyone appreciates my observations. I'd like my visit to be inconspicuous."

"I see. Then why'd you come here?"

"Professional courtesy. And I might need to ask for

a favor. You see, like you said, Brokeheart is a small town and I would like to sample some of the cultural opportunities I've heard so much about. Perhaps a visit to the opera? Could that be arranged?"

"I do see. I've just hired a new reporter to cover the social events that have become so much a part of Leadville. I'll have him show you around."

The editor opened the door and called out, "Send Tobias in here." Then to me, "We brought him all the way from Chicago. Stole him away, really. I think you'll find him interesting, and he knows everything that happens along Harrison Avenue."

A perfumery smell teased at my nose. The door opened and I looked up at Landry's dandy.

"Elicott Tobias." He shook my hand.

My mother had taught me two things. First, when a situation turns gritty, look a man in the eye and smile. He will think you know more than you do.

"Call me Kepler. Pleased to meet you." I fought the grin that threatened to curl the corners of my lips.

The other thing my mother taught me was to make sure there is a bit of fact in your lies. Mother said that a quarter turn on the truth is better than the tallest tale.

I looked him in the eye and said, "Your editor told me that you're from Chicago. I think I remember meeting you."

Tobias pulled his hand away. "I'm sure I would have remembered."

"I'll let you two figure that out later," Thomas said. "Tobias, Kepler is that reporter from Brokeheart that's been writing all those stories on how the big boys treat the poor miners. He's going to be here for a few days checking on things out at the mines. While he's here I'd like you to show him around and give him a taste of all Leadville's got to offer these days."

"No doubt," I continued to smile, "You're probably tired. Late night with the opera and parties and all. Meeting your deadline. Why don't I buy your dinner? I hear the food is very good at the Delaware Hotel."

Tobias looked at Thomas, then back at me. He shifted his weight from one foot to the other. "I need to get back to something. I'll meet you at the Delaware at eight." And he left the room.

Thomas' eyebrow arched. The unlit cigar drooped from his mouth. "Kepler, if it's not too early, would you like a drink?" He found two glasses and a whiskey bottle in a desk drawer.

I let out a deep breath. "I could use one."

Thomas drained his whiskey in a single gulp. He struck a match on the sole of his boot and lit his cigar. "That's the fewest words I've heard Tobias say since I've known the man." He filled his glass again. "Now tell me what all that was about."

"I'm not sure what you–"

"You come waltzin' into my office talking about professional courtesy. Next thing I know you and Tobias are eyeing each other like a pair of banty roosters." He blew a cloud of smoke out of the side of his mouth. "I've been in this business long enough to guess you smell a story. If it's in my town, I want a piece of it."

Thomas leaned across his desk and breathed the next lungful of smoke in my face. "What are you doing here?"

I took a sip of my whiskey and considered what portion

of the truth to share with the editor. My fingertips twirled my glass on his desktop. "I'm being followed," I said.

In the next ten minutes I spun a tale of the events at the Months. Madison's dislike of me. And how Oscar and Hayden had followed me to Leadville. I finished my story and said, "I know that Madison has connections with the mines here. I thought if it appeared that I was working with your paper, it would give me credibility and a measure of safety."

Thomas splashed more whiskey in his glass. "And what about Tobias? You two know each other?"

"I'm sure I've seen him somewhere before this morning."

He shook his head. "I can make sure you're introduced to the right people up at the mines. I'll let the police know to keep an eye out for the two you think are following you. And you're going to do one favor for me."

"What do you need?"

"Keep an eye on Tobias. I don't trust that fancy."

I held out my glass for more whiskey. Thomas sloshed a bit in my glass and filled his to the top.

"You see, Kepler, there're some rumors goin' 'round about rich folk and late-night parties that go to near dawn. They found themselves some kind of spooky leader. Tobias is right smack-dab in the middle of it. If it was just drinkin' and women, I wouldn't give it another thought. Bored rich folks."

He reached for the bottle, then pulled his hand back.

"Then the bodies started showin' up."

"Bodies? Someone was killed?"

Thomas held up three fingers. "First some drifter was found behind the assay office."

I remembered the article in the newspaper I had taken from June.

"The next night, a washerwoman out behind the railyards," Thomas continued. "And just three days ago, police found an old miner along the creek. I saw all three bodies. It looked like some animal tore all hell out of them."

"What makes you think Tobias and his group of rich people have anything to do with it?"

Red veins webbed his eyes. "Just a feeling down deep in my gut. Nose around and see what you think."

I wanted to tell Thomas about the bodies in Brokeheart. Show the newspaper accounts and postmarks on Nicolae's letters that established a pattern of killing. But I had built a tangled web of half-truths and decided to let these events play their course.

"I didn't see anything in your paper about the killings," I said.

"The police claim they were accidents and a coyote got to the bodies before they were found. If it had been one of those fancies, they'd be a singing a different tune." He dropped the stub of the cigar on the floor and ground it out with his boot heel. "Get friendly with Tobias. Get invited to one of those parties. See where it leads."

Chapter Twelve

Pale blue skies hurried away the morning clouds. I walked through wisps of ground fog as gray as the editor's cigar smoke, floating low over the muddy streets. At the Little Pittsburg Mine offices, I spent most of an hour waiting to talk to a manager about the pending strike, but he left me cooling my heels. I excused myself and told the woman in the office I would be back the next day.

I wandered the town's side streets, always careful to watch for Hayden and Oscar, and found my way to the livery stables. Seer pawed the floor of his stall as I came near. I led him into the cool morning. For the next hour, I curried my horse. Seer slurped sugar from my palm. I flipped a half dollar to a grinning stable boy to ensure the horse got an extra ration of grain.

Outside my boarding house window, daylight trickled away until a knife edge of orange outlined the western mountains. I scribbled a few notes to send to Brokeheart, then unloaded my pistol, wiped each cartridge with a clean cloth, and reloaded the weapon. I changed into a clean shirt for my dinner with Tobias. Instead of tucking the pistol in my belt, I dropped it into my coat pocket.

Again, I took to the back streets. Night shadows erased the boldness I'd had in the daylight and my senses pulled whipcord tight. Woodsmoke drifted from chimneys. Muted noise from rowdies in the saloons along Harrison Avenue floated on the air. I fastened the last few buttons on my coat against the cold and joined the crowds along the main street.

The air thickened. The smoke odor turned pungent. Others around me noticed it, too. Almost as one, men raised arms and pointed to a faint shimmer over the warehouses and corrals near the train yards. Saloons emptied onto the boardwalks.

As if something from another world demanded it, yellow flames catapulted into the darkness.

"It's the stables!" a voice cried.

I scrambled with the rush toward the burning building. Fire burst from the loft. Wide-eyed animals bunched against the fence slats in the corral next to the barn. A pinto, fighting to escape the terror, bared its teeth and snapped at the flanks of the nearest horse. That animal reared and flung itself over the back of another.

Fence rails splintered under the horses' weight and they charged out of the precious opening. As the terrified pinto lunged for safety, a jagged end of a broken board impaled the horse's white belly. It screamed as ropes of its own intestines uncoiled onto the dirt and were smashed by a dozen fleeing hooves.

"Seer!" I screamed.

The barn's doors pitched open. The stable boy I'd seen just hours before stumbled from the hellhole tugging at the halter of a thrashing gray stallion. The boy lost his footing and tumbled to the ground. Fire sprang from his coat. The boy's arms flailed in a useless attempt to swat the flames that burned at his back. In an instant the boy's hair ignited into bright red ringlets.

The stallion, now free, pivoted on its rear legs and sprinted headlong back into the blazing barn.

A man dressed for the opera pushed by me, pulling a long cape from his shoulders. He swung the garment over the screaming boy. Other men joined and beat the fire away.

Every gap in the stable's rough lumber siding blazed red. Anguished screams as from the very pit of hell rose above the inferno as dying horses burned in their stalls.

The roof collapsed. Sparks lifted a hundred feet in the air. Burning cinders showered the ground.

The crowd pushed in around me.

"Save the town!"

"Stay back!"

"Join in!"

Order emerged in all the chaos. Police pushed the crowd back. They herded me into a line with the other men. A bucket of water was handed man-to-man down the line. Then another. In minutes I was part of a chain, moving water to the fire. Two policemen with wooden poles moved close and pushed the still-burning stable walls down on the fiery center.

The biggest of the policemen marched down the line as we passed the buckets. "It's too late for those poor animals. Keep that water coming, boys. We'll not let it spread."

Flames crackled, then sizzled with each splash of water. Heat scorched the side of my face closest to the fire. My numb fingers clawed at each new pail that passed by. A gunshot cracked above the roar of the flames. I turned just as the disemboweled pinto thrashed its last. The big policeman tucked his pistol away.

White ashes floated from the black sky and settled onto the shoulders of my coat. I handed the last bucket to the nameless man next to me. The stench of singed hair and burnt meat was all around me. What had been the stable glowed like red-hot steel.

My shoulders slumped from exhaustion. Tears for Seer spilled down my cheeks. Soot streaked my hands and I felt it on my face. My confused thoughts piled one on top of another like the crumpled building.

Three men fell to the ground next to empty buckets. People who had hurried from Harrison Avenue milled at the edge of the dim light from the barn's embers. I spotted the silhouette of Madison's big man, Hayden. A cigarette glowed red in his lips. Oscar stepped out of the alley behind him. He swung a whiskey bottle to his mouth and gulped the liquor down. His lips curled back over his rat-like teeth as he smiled. He touched a finger to his tongue and pointed at me. Hayden took the bottle and the two men walked into the dark alleyway. I watched until the speck of light from Hayden's cigarette disappeared.

"Kepler?" A man's voice called to me. "Kepler, that you?"

I glanced toward the words.

The man spoke again. "Kepler, it's me, Thomas, from the paper."

My hand still held the pistol in my pocket. I looked back at the alley once more.

"You see what happened here?" Thomas asked.

I rubbed the back of my hand across my face. "I followed the crowd down here when it first flared up."

"You write a story, I'll print it. None of my people got here until it was near out. I sent one of mine over to the doctor's to see about the boy. Heard he was burned pretty bad. Talked to the owner. He thinks there were six or eight horses inside when it went up."

"One of them was mine."

Thomas shook his head. "Damn shame. But coulda been so much worse. A gust of wind from the right direction and the whole town might've gone with it." He pushed a flat bottle into my hand. "Looks like you can use some of this."

I took a long drink.

Thomas reached for the bottle and nodded at the crowd still in the street. "Did you see them? Tobias and his friends must've thought this was more entertaining than one of their parties."

Tobias stood in the center of the group. Just behind his shoulder, I saw Landry's face and dark hair. She took his arm in both her hands and cocked her head. Nicolae stood by himself a few steps from the cluster, his back to the scene. He tapped a walking stick on the boardwalk.

"They were right there when I got here," Thomas said. "Never moved, not one of them. None even tried to help." He took another swig. "Damnedest thing was—" He looked away. "When that horse tore its guts out, I'd swear that dark-haired woman laughed."

I jerked my head around. Landry walked toward Harrison Street, still on Tobias's arm. She swiveled her head around for a last look at the burned building and dead horses, then walked away with her group of friends.

"Not much more we can do here tonight. Meet me at my office early. I talked to the chief of police." Thomas gestured with the bottle toward the broad-shouldered man who had organized the bucket brigade. "He told me the owner claims somebody broke in and started the fire."

Thomas shrugged. "We'll pay both of them a visit. Now get yourself some rest. You look terrible."

Chapter Thirteen

An icy rim on the frozen mud crunched under my boots. Ghostly wisps of smoke rose in a dozen places from the black rubble of the burned stable. Frost shimmered on the dead pinto's stiff carcass.

Thomas caught the sleeve of my jacket and pointed to a stoop-shouldered man near the charred ruins. Strands of hair whipped in the breeze over his bowed head. The man's hat hung in his hands.

"Jorgensen," Thomas said softly, as if he didn't want to disturb a prayer. "Jorgensen." A bit louder.

The man turned his face toward us, but there was no recognition in his red-rimmed eyes.

"Jorgensen, Sam Thomas from the newspaper. Remember me? I bought a horse from you last spring."

Jorgensen turned back to the black pile that had been his stable. "Men make plans and God laughs." His chest heaved as he drew in a deep breath. "I's goin' ta sell this place, I was. No more, I tell ya. Mother and me was goin' back home. Away from dis dirty town. Not no more."

"I'm sorry," Thomas said and glanced at me.

"God willed it. Nothin' just happens, ya know. I was over to the mill. Ordered lumber and tings. I build it up again, I will."

"Jorgensen," I said. "My name's Kepler. I met you day before yesterday. I brought my horse—"

"Ya, I remember. You pay extra for stall. Red horse, white face. Eyes, one brown, other blue."

"Seer," I said. "My horse's name was Seer."

"I see him before I leave last night, I do."

"Well, that's—that's, ah. We wanted to talk to you about what the sheriff said. Did he say anything about someone starting the fire?"

"God willed it." Jorgensen spread his arms. "Next I build bigger. More stalls. Bigger corral."

I glanced sideways at Thomas. He shook his head and motioned for me to follow him. I looked back at Jorgensen and was about to tell him goodbye.

Jorgensen turned his face toward the sky. His arms dropped to his sides and his hat fell from his fingers onto the ashes at his feet. "Kepler," he said. "Your horse. He down by river. Men find him with others that ran 'way."

I stepped forward. "Are you sure?" I felt my voice rise. "He was in the barn. In his stall."

"Good horse. He know what would happen. Somehow—"

"Jorgensen," I shouted. "Is my horse alive?"

"Yes." He looked at me with eyes that didn't see.

The burden I wouldn't admit was there slipped from my shoulders and I ran for the river. Mud caked my boots as I crossed the trampled remains of the corral. I hurtled through the splintered boards where the horses had found their escape, then crossed the railroad tracks to the edge of town. My feet shot out from under me on the frost-slick grass at the river bank. I fell onto my hip and slid to the water's edge.

Seer nickered nearby.

A loop of rope knotted to his bridle tethered him to a

tree. Soot streaked his white face. He tossed his head and strained at the cord.

I splashed into the running water. Eight other horses pawed the ground and tugged at their halters. Seer strained at the rope. I caught hold of his head and touched my forehead to his face.

"Seer." His name trembled from my lips. My chest jerked and a lump rose in my throat. "You're the only thing that is really mine." I could not make any more words come. In that long minute, I listened to the air fill and empty from his lungs and the thump of each heartbeat.

Thomas's boots splashed into the river behind me.

I lifted my face and stroked down the horse's neck. Knotted into his mane just above his withers, my fingers found a piece of rolled paper, no bigger than a playing card, tied with a purple ribbon. I untangled the package and slipped it into my jacket pocket as Thomas stepped up beside me.

"Damn lucky, Kepler." He reached out and patted Seer's back. "After all that last night, bet you thought you'd never see him again. Tell you what. Take him over to my place. Put him in the corral with my two. My boy'll watch after him until you leave town."

Thomas gave me directions to his house. I promised to meet him back at the newspaper office. Thomas left and I led Seer to the river to drink.

As my horse stood knee-deep in the icy water, I fumbled with the note someone had tied in his mane. I recognized the handwriting.

Kepler,
I am disappointed that you didn't tell me you were here.

Meet tonight at midnight near the river where you found your horse.

Nicolae

Cold from the river seeped up my legs and stalled in the pit of my stomach.

Bell, the chief of police, straddled the chair across from Thomas's desk. The lawman wiped his face with hands still black with soot. "I've been up all night. I walked around what was left of that stable more'n a dozen times jus' lookin' for somethin' that might give me a clue to what really happened. Ol' Jorgensen swears that he don't allow no lanterns in the stable and that the hired boy is careful."

Thomas took a full whiskey bottle from the bottom drawer of his desk. He held it up and raised his eyebrows.

I shook my head.

Bell said, "Hell, yes." He reached for one of the glasses and held it for Thomas to fill. "I'm goin' home and gettin' some sleep after this. Whiskey'll help take the edge off."

"Did you find anything?" I asked.

"Maybe, but I don't want any of this in tonight's paper." He looked at Thomas.

"I've always honored our arrangement. I won't go to print with anything until you give the okay," Thomas said.

"Can I trust him?" Bell motioned toward me with the whiskey glass.

"I vouch for him," Thomas said.

Bell raised his face toward mine and stared at me with rheumy eyes. He emptied the glass without looking away.

"It might be nothin'," he began. "I talked with the stable boy early this mornin'. He's not as bad off as I thought.

Doc says the burns will heal up and most of his hair will grow back."

The lawman set the empty glass on Thomas's desk. "Anyways, the boy swears he heard voices at the back of the stable before the fire went up. The ground is all tore up out front, but on the back side of what's left of that buildin', I found two sets of boot tracks. One set musta been from a big fella." He held out his two hands. The space he measured was over a foot. "The boot heels sunk down deep in the mud. The other tracks're only half that size. They led up to a back window like someone was lookin' in at the horses and then walked away." Bell rubbed the palms of his hands on his dirty trouser legs. "I backtracked the footprints a mite and there was tobacco and makin's scattered on the ground. Like somebody mighta rolled one."

"And tossed a lit cigarette butt into the stable?" I asked.

"Appeared so." The sheriff looked at Thomas and then back at me. "There's a couple of new fellas hangin' 'round town here. The little 'un's got a sharp face and dark eyes. Kinda like a rat. The other 'un's a big man. Near twice the size of his partner. Big one's always got a smoke in his teeth. You know anythin' about those boys, Kepler?"

Thomas's chair creaked.

"Sounds like the two that followed me here from Brokeheart."

"If you got trouble with them two, take it out of my town. I've got enough of my own without you importin' any more."

"Look here, Bell," Thomas broke in. "You said yourself that it only appeared . . . You can't be sure of any of this."

"I'm sure that those two been askin' about Kepler. Did

they start the fire at Jorgenson's? No way to be sure. I'm just sayin' if Kepler here is about done with his business in town, it might be better for all of us." Bell looked at me. "What's it gonna be?"

I spoke before Thomas could protest. "I have a meeting tonight. By tomorrow morning, I will be able to tell you how much longer I'll stay."

The sheriff eyed me. "I guess one more day won't matter. Be expectin' some sorta answer in the morning." He pulled himself off the chair and tipped his head toward Thomas. "I'm holdin' you to our agreement. Nothin' in the paper, hear me?"

Thomas waited until the sheriff closed the office door behind him. "You think the fire was some sort of message for you?"

"I would say there's a connection." A portrait of old Jorgenson standing in front of his burned stable painted itself on my mind.

"Damn."

"Yeah, damn. I'm going to the bank and have some money wired up from my account in Brokeheart. You see it gets to Jorgenson. Don't use my name." I stood up. "Let me use a desk when I get back, I'll write the story you wanted on the fire. Make it a desk close to Tobias. We missed our dinner appointment last night."

No sooner had I stepped from the newspaper office to the street when Chief Bell stormed up the boardwalk. He grabbed the front of my jacket and pulled me close.

"So help me, if this is any of your doin's, I'll run you out of town before . . ." he said through clenched teeth.

"What are you talking about?"

His grip eased ever so slightly. He cocked his head.

"Thomas's fancy reporter. They found him dead. Upstairs at the Delaware."

I pushed his hands away. "What happened?"

"I'm fixin' on finding that out, right now."

Thomas pushed into the room ahead of me. The desk clerk, Collier, pressed his back to the window frame. His good hand scratched at the stump of his severed arm. His face was pale and the cuff of his pants was wet with the vomit that pooled on his shoe tops.

The perfume from Tobias's curls hung in the sour smell that filled the room. The dead man's hair spread across the pillow and his sightless eyes studied the ceiling.

"Collier. Collier! Look at me when I talk," Bell said in a hoarse whisper.

The clerk lifted his face to the lawman and then dropped his chin on his chest. "I'm sick," he muttered.

"Just tell me again what you know."

"Mr. Tobias came down from the party–"

"What party?"

Collier looked away and his eyes found me. "Most nights there's this late party. After the opera. Some people meet here and–"

"What people, boy?"

"Some rich people from here in town. That's all I know."

"Go on."

"Mr. Tobias came down 'bout two in the mornin'. Said he needed a room. Wanted to spend the night instead of goin' home. Said he wanted a room facin' the alley. I gave him a key. That's all I know." He pulled in a ragged breath. "Can I leave?"

"No." Bell looked at me. "Shut that door."

Collier half turned toward the window. He twisted his head as if he needed to peek at Tobias, and then spun his face back to glass.

Bell motioned for Thomas and me to come closer to the bed where the body lay. "See the bruises on his neck? I betcha it's broke." The sheriff's hands trembled as he grabbed the bedsheet and moved it back. "But look at this. Like a half-cleaned deer."

The skin had been ripped away from the bottom of the ribs to the man's crotch. Intestines, stomach, and kidneys spilled onto the sheet. *Like the horse at the fire. Like the bodies on the mountain above Nicolae's lodge.*

Bell pulled the sheet over the dead man's face. "No knife blade slashed him open like that. And there's hardly any blood. Like something lapped it up."

Collier emptied his stomach on the window glass.

Bell grabbed Collier's good arm and jerked him to the bedside. Tears flooded down the clerk's face.

"Tell me what you know or I'll shove your face in his belly." Bell's meaty hand clamped on the clerk's neck and pushed down. Collier gagged and tried to wrench away from Bell's grip.

Collier cried, "I told you. He came for the room key."

"Tell me everythin' you know about these late-night parties." Bell pushed Collier's head closer to the sheet.

"That man in the fancy train car. He's the leader."

Bell pushed harder.

"Let him go!" I took hold of the sheriff's wrist and

tugged his hand away from the man's neck. Bell jerked his hand back and balled a fist, ready to strike at me.

"Collier," I said without taking my eyes from the sheriff. "Take a minute and collect yourself." Bell's arm dropped to his side. "Nobody's accusing you of anything. Just explain to the sheriff what you know about the parties and how Tobias was involved." I forced a calm evenness in my voice.

Collier retreated to his place by the stained window. He propped the stump of his arm against the plaster and mopped his face with his hand.

"They–those rich folks–used to come into the hotel after the opera. The men would go in the bar and drink. Smoke their cigars. Their women would set in the lobby and talk among theirselves. About two months ago, that fella with the train car showed up here. All dressed up fancy and everything."

I handed Collier my handkerchief. He wiped his eyes and face. He looked at his mess on the floor and turned back to the window. "Tobias asked me first. They wanted a private room. On the next floor there's a three-room suite that the mine people use when someone important comes to town. It just sets empty most of the time." He wadded my kerchief in his fingers.

"There's 'bout ten of 'em. More men than women. I'd get the liquor they wanted. They made me swear to keep what they did up there secret."

The sheriff broke in, "Just what did they do?"

I raised my hand to quiet Bell. "Go on, Collier."

"They was up there 'most every night. None of 'em work 'cept Mr. Tobias. They live on the money their daddies made.

"After awhile they wanted more than just whiskey. Tobias asked me to get that opium stuff from the Chinaman. Then they wanted those girls from the cribs down by the station. They said if I ever said anything they'd—" Collier wheezed. "Paid me real good to keep quiet."

He began to sob. "Man like me with one arm," he raised the stump, "won't never be much. Their money was my chance."

Like Nicolae's promises were mine.

"Who's this man with the train car you're talkin' about?" Bell asked.

"I know him," I said. "Remember back at Thomas's office I told you, Sheriff, I had a meeting tonight? Nicolae wants to see me."

"Nicolae?"

"Send Collier away. He won't talk. And I'll tell you everything I know."

"One more thing." Collier looked at me. "It wasn't the first night Mr. Tobias took a room here. He was real friendly with that woman that lives with that man. He called her Landry. Everybody else would leave except Tobias and her. I'd see her sneak out before sunup. She scares me. There was something about her eyes." With that, Collier bolted out the door.

When I finished telling my story to Bell and Thomas, I said, "I think it's best if I go alone. I'll see what Nicolae has to say."

"I don't like this one bit." Thomas shook his head.

I looked at the sheriff. "We got no proof he's involved in this at all. What Collier said means nothing."

"You're right," Bell nodded. "All we have is that cripple's story about parties and Tobias takin' a room. Even if you can get this Nicolae to admit he killed Tobias, he'd deny it later. It'd be your word against his." The sheriff paused. "You sure you want to be there at midnight?"

I nodded and left the room.

"You're a brave man or a fool." The sheriff's words followed me out the door.

I'd played enough cards to know when a man's luck is about to run out. At the bank I made arrangements for two hundred dollars to be sent to Thomas. I left a note to go with the money asking Thomas to see that the stable owner got the money. I asked that the rest of the money I'd earned from the newspaper stories and Nicolae be transferred to a small account I maintained in Cheyenne.

I stopped at a general store and bought a bit of brown sugar for Seer. Then I went to the depot and checked the schedule. There was only one train to Denver that day. It was scheduled to leave at ten minutes to midnight. I bought a ticket.

Chapter Fourteen

The woman's lonely eyes stared back at me from the tintype picture pasted inside the cover of my watch. That woman, my mother, many times had told me that what others say about you should never determine the path you choose. For most of my life I thought those words were her own way of justifying the choices she had made. Even after the income from the boarding house and laundry she owned provided security, she continued to climb the stairs at the Painted Lantern Parlor on the arm of one of the dandies who gathered there.

"Son," she told me the night I fled the town that would forever label me as the whore's bastard child, "complications are a part of life. Running from them only postpones the decisions until some other time or some other place." She pressed a bundle wrapped in one of her lace kerchiefs into my hands. "I decided that I would not run anymore. Someday you may have to make that same choice."

There were two hundred dollars in that package and an ivory-handled pistol. The money was gone before the month was over. That gun was in my coat pocket now.

I pressed my back against the rough wood siding of the depot building and checked my pocket watch. In ten minutes the last train would leave for Denver. In ten more, Nicolae would be at the river waiting for me.

I took a deep breath and considered the events that had

brought me to this particular moment in my life. My money would be safe in the Cheyenne bank by the time I reached Denver. As my eyes clenched tight, the maimed bodies of the hanged woman, the captain, the two men on the mountain, and Tobias visited my mind once more.

My lucky streak had played out. At least, in Colorado. Word was that the Montana Territory would be the next boom. When I'd jumped off the freight wagon in Brokeheart, my pockets were empty. Now I had money. All I would leave behind would be Seer. Thomas seemed a good man. I would send a letter asking him to care for the horse.

The conductor called, "All aboard."

My tongue traced a circle on the inside of my cheek.

Complications are a part of life.

I plucked the train ticket from my coat and let it flutter away in the night breeze. Mother's "someday" was here.

I crossed the wooden platform and jumped down onto the frozen railyard. A patchwork of clouds pressed down over the streets and buildings. Steel-blue light slipped between the seams in the clouds, stealing away all but the grayest shadows. I paused, then sprinted across the tracks to the top of the riverbank and listened to the water below me. The cold breeze stung my nose, the hint of tobacco smoke floated on the air.

Hayden and Oscar?

Since I had found that scrap of paper tied to Seer's mane, I had used every spare thought to rehearse the things I would say to Nicolae.

I had forgotten about Madison's hired killers.

I pressed myself against a lone, twisted cottonwood across the river from the stand of trees where I'd found Seer that morning. Scanning the blackness for any movement, I prayed the sounds of the river would drown out the thumps of my heart.

The locomotive coughed and a whoosh of steam filled the night. Tracks rattled and the train I could have been on left for Denver. Light swirled from the steam engine's headlamp. A little man in the bowler hat darted across the tracks and dropped into a bend in the riverbed a hundred yards upstream from where I waited.

I pressed tighter against the tree's rough bark and wrestled the pistol from my coat. The clatter of the train faded. The splash and spill of water over river rocks made the only sounds in the empty night.

The orange speck of Hayden's cigarette betrayed the big man. He picked his way through the trees on the other side of the river. A rifle hung in the crook of his elbow. He stopped, turned an ear toward me, and then with three quick jerks of his hand motioned for Oscar to move forward.

The rounded hat appeared above the river bank. Oscar ran a half-dozen steps and dropped on one knee. He tugged back his duster and pulled the long-barreled Colt from its holster.

They knew I was somewhere along this river. The tree at my back hid me. If I tried to run for the station buildings I would need to cross the open railyards. A move toward the shelter of the forest would mean crossing the knee-deep river.

Hayden had closed the distance between us to fifty yards. An easy shot for a man with a rifle. The hide-out pistol in my hand had served well across a poker table, but it was no match for Hayden's saddle gun.

Oscar splashed along the edge of the water. He took

a few steps and squatted below the gully's rim. He nudged the brim of his hat with the barrel of his revolver.

Hayden whistled to his partner. "Like huntin' rabbits," he said boldly. "We'll just keep pushin' this way 'til he flushes."

Oscar's squeaky voice called back, "Last I saw he was runnin' toward that lone tree on my side of the water. I'm gonna circle out a mite and ease up on it. Keep that Winchester ready, hear me?"

Hayden lunged through a tangle of brush to the riverbank. I felt his eyes search the edges of the shadows that the tree cast. The rifle's butt touched his shoulder, ready at any second to send a bullet my way.

Moonlight sliced the dark clouds. Its silvery brightness cascaded over the ripples in the water at my feet. I dared not turn my head. My eyes followed Oscar, then glanced back to Hayden on the opposite riverbank.

"Gotta be sittin' tight in the shadows of that old tree," Oscar squealed. "I'm gonna fire a couple shots in there. Be ready if'n he runs for it."

Oscar thumbed back the hammer of the big Colt.

Throw two shots at Oscar and hope that the muzzle flash won't give away my hiding place. Then dive for the river. Fire at Hayden as I roll. It was my only plan. In the confusion I might be able to make it across to the cover of underbrush and trees. Drawing to an inside straight had better odds, but it seemed to be my only chance.

Oscar raised himself to one knee. I glanced back at Hayden. The moonlight outlined his rounded shoulders and glinted off his carbine's barrel.

Now. My muscles became spring steel.

I heard the sound before I could raise my pistol. It

crashed through the brush. Hayden screamed. His body flew to the edge of the water. A huge wolf, as black as the night, tore at the man's throat.

"Hayden!" Oscar cried out. A ragged flame leaped from the muzzle of his pistol.

A second wolf leaped from the brush. Gray streaked its black fur. The animal's front legs seemed to graze the water at the center of the river. Then its powerful hind legs hurled it toward Oscar. The gun flew from Oscar's hand. The gray wolf caught his outstretched arm and pulled him to the ground.

I pressed harder into the cover of the tree. Screams of the two men blended with the growls of the animals. An unholy chorus. Bone snapped. Hayden's body dropped from the bigger animal's jaws.

Oscar's hands clamped on the snarling beast's face. He screamed as the animal's teeth ripped at his stomach. Even in the animal's frenzy I heard some small bit of pleasure in its growls. The pitch of Oscar's screams grew louder and louder, then ceased. His killer's tongue lapped at the torn body. Then the gray wolf left Oscar and crossed the river to its companion.

The black wolf's front feet perched on Hayden's lifeless chest. Its head swung in a slow arc over its kill. The gray animal leaped from the water. It nuzzled the face of the black. Both raised their muzzles to the midnight sky in a single ghostly howl.

I will swear until the day I die that I saw their eyes glow with a purple flame.

Both sets of those eyes then found me. The smaller wolf paced the river's edge. It whimpered, as if begging the other animal to allow it to come for me. The big wolf raked its teeth over the smaller's flanks, and in a liquid blur the two disappeared into the forest.

I buried my hands in the tangle of weeds and sticks below the tree and pushed myself to my feet. My legs would not hold me. I slumped back onto my knees. I raised the pistol at the place where the wolves had run. I wanted to fire but my hands trembled so much I couldn't have hit the river bank if I'd aimed at it.

Whether it was seconds, minutes, or much longer, I'll never be sure. I heard my teeth chatter. No matter how hard I clenched my jaw, I could not stop the tremors that racked my being. Finally I pulled myself toward Oscar's broken body. The grays and blacks of the night could not hide the carnage. The darkest black marked his bloodstains in the gravel. Like Tobias, Oscar's skin had been torn away from his stomach. Spilled guts glimmered in silvery grays.

I commanded the muscles in my legs to stand. The toe of my boot tipped Oscar's derby into the river. Like a child's boat, it fled that terrible scene. The river water's icy chill did not revive any part of me. It only numbed me more.

I stumbled through the water to where Hayden's body was sprawled. His face twisted away from his massive shoulders. The flesh stretched tight over lumps of bone. Teeth marks in his neck, black with his blood, ripped his skin. My mind snapped to what I had seen on Sophia's throat at the undertaker's that day in Brokeheart. And the captain in the alleyway. The man on the mountain.

Nicolae. His note had invited me to this place. He must have seen this. Was he waiting somewhere nearby? Or had he already been here?

Warmth from the pit of my stomach rushed up my spine. The fire licked at my senses. My fingers touched the marks the wolf's paws left in the bloody soil. Smaller tracks followed the larger set into the forest beyond the river. Tucking Mother's revolver in my coat, I pried Hayden's fingers from his rifle's stock and pulled myself to my full height.

Night winds swirled the clouds. Moonlight, now free, traded pewter shades for the blacks. Somewhere in the trees, the wolves howled again.

With a dead man's rifle in my hands, I followed their tracks. I chose each step slowly, forbidding any noise from my footfalls on the icy gravel. A dozen steps, search for any sound. A dozen more, study the shadows and listen again. Each time a cloud crossed the moon, the wolves lifted their eerie cry.

I pushed tree branches away with the barrel of Hayden's gun, zigzagged around the thickest brush, and studied each tree bough that moved in the night's breezes. The forest opened to a meadow. Rocks the size of whiskey barrels lay scattered among the frosty grasses. I squatted in a tangle of juniper in the shadows of the trees and scanned the forest's edges.

The black wolf loped into the clearing. It raised its face to the sky. A low rumble rose from deep inside the animal and then burst out in a wail to the moon. The gray wolf joined the other's song with long, painful yips. The smaller animal paced the edge of the forest, refusing to step full into the open.

An inch at a time, I moved the rifle to my shoulder.

The black wolf reared up onto its hind legs. Its front paws batted at the moon. The animal's head rolled back. Its teeth snapped at some invisible enemy. Its bay turned to a horrible shriek.

Great clouds of steam flew from its nostrils and its wide

mouth. The shrill cries of the gray wolf drowned out its partner's howls.

I squinted down the barrel of the rifle. The gun sights wavered on the point of the black wolf's front shoulder. I drew in a breath, trying to calm my shaking hands. My finger tightened on the trigger.

The cloud of the animal's own breath grew thick around its face. It yelped and stretched higher, front legs reaching for the sky.

I could not hold the gun steady.

Then the wolf tumbled onto its side. The steam from its breath swirled thick around the fallen creature. A deep howl hung in the air. Louder and louder the sound came tearing at my ears. The yowl turned to a single word.

"Landry."

The gray wolf leaped from the cover of the trees. Silvery mist spilled from its mouth and nose. The vapors mingled into a single cloud. A thousand needle points of light sparkled in the moonlit haze.

The rifle dropped from my cheek.

The yowls from the fog before me were no longer the sounds of animals. A woman's scream tore the night.

As suddenly as it had all began, the wind wiped away the vapor curtain.

Some demon had entered my mind. My eyes failed me. What I saw could only be the ploy of some imp from the very pit of hell. Bile churned in my throat. The gun hung useless in my stiff hands.

Nicolae squatted in the last wisp of the steam. His bare back was toward me. One hand brushed the mane of long black hair away from his face. His thick shoulders shrugged.

He turned one eye toward the sky. His tongue licked his lips and then the back of each hand.

"Landry?" I heard his hoarse whisper.

Where the gray wolf had been, Landry sprang to her feet. Moisture glistened on her naked skin. Her eyes pulled wide and she glared down at the kneeling Nicolae. He reached for her. She stepped back. The tip of her tongue found the streaks of black blood on her hands. Nicolae reached out again. Landry's lips curled back over her teeth. She snapped a shrill barking sound. The same sound I'd heard her make at the cur dog in the train yard.

Her nostrils flared. She sniffed the air. Nicolae's knees dropped to the ground and he turned the side of his face to where I hid. His nose twitched at the scent in the air.

They smelled my fear.

"Run." Newfound strength filled his voice.

Landry hesitated. His arm touched her shoulder and in long, wolf-like strides, the two disappeared into the shadows of the forest.

I stood for a long time looking down at the footprints on the frozen grass. I wanted it to be different. I wanted to convince myself that what I had seen was a dream. Even a nightmare. But the full moon's light showed it all. The tracks of the big wolf led to the matted place on the grass. The tracks of the smaller wolf joined him there.

Barefoot tracks of a man and a woman led away, into the forest. No matter how I tried to see something different, it was there before me. Everything I had refused to let myself believe, all the puzzle pieces that I refused to put together, and everything I feared showed plainly. But who could I tell? And who would believe me if I did? This bit of proof would melt away in the morning sun.

I followed the footprints further into the forest. I pointed the rifle at every shadow that flickered in the fading moonlight. But I doubted it would be any protection against these creatures.

And there were questions. Why had Nicolae invited me to the river? Why kill Hayden and Oscar, but spare me? Why hadn't Nicolae and Landry come for me at the meadow?

Most horrifying of all: was I some tool in Nicolae's plan?

I found a scrap of material from one of the dresses I'd seen Landry wearing hanging from a limb. The footprints milled around bent trees, and when the trail began again, it showed the marks of shoes, not bare feet. And this trail led back to town.

The first light of dawn painted blood-red veins over the horizon. The streaks tore open and spilled gaudy crimson light over the new day.

A train's whistle split the air. Train cars creaked as they stretched against their couplers, then banged together in compliance with the pull of the locomotive. From the forested hill, I watched the day's first train leave Leadville. Nicolae's car was hitched in the line.

Thomas opened the back door of his house. He pushed his hand through his hair and tugged his coat tight around his chest. "That you, Kepler?"

I leaned over the top rail of the fence and rested my head on Seer's neck. Thomas's two horses tried to push in next to Seer, but my horse blocked them and guarded me for himself.

Thomas walked to where I stood. "I waited with the sheriff 'til near two. Then we both gave up. Did you find Nicolae?"

"Yeah."

"And?"

"Those two men that followed me here from Brokeheart? Tell the sheriff he can find their bodies along the river bank behind the train yard."

"Gawd, Kepler! What happened out there? You kill 'em?"

I shook my head.

"Nicolae, then?"

"Wolves." I bit down on my lip and stroked Seer's face.

"Wolves killed two full-grown men and you saw it happen?"

"Don't ask me more." I didn't look up and continued to stroke Seer. "Nicolae's car was part of the train that just left town. Any idea where it was headed?"

Thomas reached over the fence and grabbed a handful of one of his horse's manes. "It drops some supplies for the mines at the foot of the pass, then on to Fairplay. It'll be in Brokeheart by nightfall." He pulled his hand away from his horse and grabbed the top rail with both hands. "What happened out there?"

"Evil," I whispered.

"Sure as the turnin' of the earth, they're things out there I'll never understand." He waited for me to say more. When I didn't, he let out long slow breath. "Get on in the house and get some breakfast in ya. Your saddle got burned up in the fire. I'll put one of mine on your horse. You're headed back to Brokeheart, aren't you?"

I turned my face to Thomas. “I’m going to play this out ’til no cards are left in the deck.”

After breakfast I tucked the dead man’s rifle into the holster lashed to the borrowed saddle. I stopped at the boarding house and picked up the rest of my things. Seer sensed where we were going. We left Leadville and started down the steep trail to Brokeheart. Back to where all this began.

Chapter Fifteen

Winter wind stung my eyes. Mist from my breath clung like icy daggers from my mustache. Seer held his head low and plodded into Brokeheart. He never missed a step, never complained, the whole way off the mountain. It was as if he knew I needed rest. The wind cut through my canvas coat and numbed my body. Bloody visions numbed my mind.

I pulled Seer's saddle off and rubbed his back and legs with new straw. He stood easy in his stall. I stroked his ears as he ate two rations of grain. Though I wanted to hold on to this little peace with my horse, nightfall would bring the train from Leadville.

I left Thomas's saddle and my things in the stable with Seer. With Hayden's saddle gun over my shoulder, I set off to find the one man in Brokeheart who might help make some sense out this wickedness that tangled all around me.

Joe Medicine Pony had first warned me that evil's presence hung over this town. Sheriff Beard would know where I could find the Indian.

Despite the cold, the door to the sheriff's office stood open. Beard looked up from the open Bible on his desk. "Made it back, I see," he said. He tilted back on his chair. "Saw the story you wrote for the Leadville paper 'bout the stable fire." He cocked his head. "You look plumb wore out, Kepler. When was the last time you slept?"

His words forced the burden of the night and long trail down on me. "Doesn't matter. Where can I find Joe?"

"You got two problems."

"Did something happen to the Indian?"

"Madison put him on the payroll over to the mine. And Madison don't take too kindly to you." Beard took a paper from underneath his Bible. "But you and me need to talk about this. Telegraph from the sheriff in Leadville. Wants a statement from you about two dead men."

I looked at the paper and back at Beard.

"Madison's gunmen?" he asked.

"I didn't kill them."

"Think Madison will believe that? He sent them boys after you. You come back and they turn up dead." He shook his head. "Kepler, Madison's holding a grudge over what you put in the papers 'bout him. He ain't the kind of man you need to cross."

"Sheriff, there's more to it that–"

Beard held up a hand. "There's somethin' else you should know. When the runner brought the telegram here, he told me he was takin' another to Madison. I should be tellin' you to put that carbine away, but you might be needin' it." Beard rubbed his face. "I can only do so much. You should know this, too: Madison's been hittin' the bottle awful hard."

Beard picked up his axe handle and left for his evening rounds. I promised him that I would go to my room at the hotel and get some sleep. But two shrieks of the train whistle made me break that promise. I hurried to the station house and then cut through the corrals to where I could see the train. Three yardmen off-loaded freight from a boxcar onto a waiting wagon.

The flat gray light of dusk washed over the town. The air turned a thick sepia tone. The flames of the torches did little to add color or light. One by one, I squinted at the train cars on the tracks. But the polished wood of Nicolae's ornate car was not there. Somewhere between here and Leadville, Nicolae had decided to wait. Maybe for me.

Relief, even if temporary, pushed back my fatigue. The one constant in the last few days had been my memory of that night in the girl's room above the Months Saloon. I could still remember my fingers on the cool skin at the nape of her neck. I told myself that I needed to be sure June was safe.

Flickering light from coal-oil lamps spilled onto the street from the saloon. Two men stood at the bar and three railroaders shared what was left of a bottle around a table just inside the doorway. May spotted me and spilled whiskey into two glasses. She met me at an empty table and motioned for me to sit. I dropped in the straight-backed chair and laid the rifle across the tabletop. She put one tumbler in front of me and downed hers in a single gulp.

One of the men at the bar dropped a few coins next to his glass, pulled up the collar of his coat and nodded at the other. Both men left the barroom.

"Damn it, Kepler," May whispered and her jowls shook. "Those two boys work for Madison. Been hangin' 'round here most of the afternoon. You show up and they hightail it outta here. Any fool knows where they're headin." She shook her head. "True you killed Hayden and Oscar in Leadville?"

"They're dead, but I didn't kill 'em."

I reached for my whiskey, but May slapped my hand and drained the glass herself.

"Better git outta here, while you gotta chance."

Sounds of a man's laugh came from upstairs. A cowboy, not much older than June, stood in an open door. He put his hat on and knotted a piece of rope around the waist of his blanket coat. Outlined by a candle's light, June stepped from the door, reached up and pinched the cowboy's ear. He laughed louder and turned toward the stairs. June smiled until she saw me.

Her hands shot up and covered her face. A cry escaped through her fingers. The cowboy cranked his head at June, then back to the barroom below. He saw me staring back at him, and no doubt the Winchester on the table. He pulled at the brim of his hat and hurried down the stairs and out the front door without looking up.

One of June's hands clutched the wall next to the doorway of the upstairs room where she had led me just a week ago. I couldn't see her face, but I heard her sob.

Without thinking, I was on my feet. May caught hold of the sleeve of my coat. I pulled away, grabbed for the banister and started up the stairs. The door to June's room slammed shut.

A man's laughed boomed behind me.

"Still chasin' after that little chippy, Kepler?"

I knew the voice.

Madison's bootheels clomped into the saloon.

"This don't concern you at all, Madison," May snapped. "You ain't welcome in my—"

As I turned from the stairway, a hawk-faced man grabbed May by the arms and wrestled his forearm across her throat.

"Hold 'er tight, Jonesy. I'll bet she's full of fight."

Madison pulled open his coat. A Colt pistol was tucked in his belt.

The three railroad men bolted from their table and pushed their way out the front door. A long-haired, dark-skinned man moved into the doorway as they hurried out and sneered at me. A foot-long Bowie knife hung on his left hip.

Madison picked the rifle off the table. "This is all the proof I need," he said. "Took this offa Hayden after you killed him, didn't ya, Kepler?" He held the gun up to the light from the oil lamps on the chandelier and ran his fingers over the wood. "Hayden scratched his name in the stock with a ten-penny nail. I can see it right here."

My arms fell useless to my sides. "I didn't kill your men, Madison. They would have killed me, though. But . . ."

"But what, Kepler? You gonna try to tell me that wolves killed 'em? What kinda story is that? Writer for a newspaper and all. You can do better than that. You made up some mean stories 'bout me and how I treat miners."

May fought Jonesy's grasp. Her teeth flashed and she bit down on the back of the hand around her neck. The man jerked his arm away and yelped.

Madison took two quick steps and cracked May across the face with the rifle barrel. She fell to her hands and knees. Drops of blood fell from her mouth.

I started toward them. Madison leveled the rifle at my stomach and thumbed the hammer to full cock.

"This fat old woman'll be no help tonight, Kepler."

"Whatever you got against me has nothing to do with May."

"Judas Priest, Kepler," he slurred. "I'm going to enjoy this all I can."

Madison flipped a silver dollar into the blood on the floor near May's fingers. "May, that's for the whore. I want my man there to have a go at June. That's her name, isn't it?"

May raised her head. "Burn in hell," she said as blood dribbled from her split lip.

"Joaquin," Madison said, tilting his head to the man at the door. "Go upstairs. Visit June." Then to me, "He's good with that knife, he is."

Madison's eyes held my stare. My pistol was deep in my coat pocket. Any move to get to it would be useless.

Joaquin pulled the knife from his belt and wiped the blade on the leg of his pants. He came toward the stairway.

I prayed June would slip out the window. I could lunge for Madison. A bullet from the Winchester would kill me. But from the look in Madison's eyes, he wanted someone to suffer. If I was dead, May and her girls would pay.

The stairs creaked under Joaquin's weight. Madison's lips curled in a smile. I heard the latch on the door of June's room open. Madison glanced up.

May edged toward his legs. She lifted her face and through the bloody lips mouthed the word, "Now."

A blur of flame flashed behind me. Joaquin screamed with pain.

May threw her bulk against Madison's knees. I dove forward at Madison, grabbing the barrel of the rifle and pushing it away. Madison tumbled over May. The front sight of the Winchester caught on my sleeve as he yanked the trigger. The blast tore at my coat and burned the flesh of my arm. With all I had in me, I wrenched the gun from his hands.

May spun from her place on the floor, snatched a whiskey glass from the table and smashed it into Madison's face.

From the corner of my eye I saw Joaquin stumble from the stairs with his shirt and long hair in flames. His mouth was open, but he could make no noise.

The hulking Jonesy lurched toward me. I swung the rifle with both hands. He lifted his arms to ward off the blow. I saw the raw marks from May's teeth on his hand as the gunstock splintered on his face. In mid-stride his body went limp and he dropped onto the floor.

Madison, still on his back, hurled May away from his face and clawed for the six-gun in his belt. I brought the broken stock down like a spear, like I was the wolf, wanting only to kill. The jagged end found his throat. Bone and gristle snapped. Blood flooded up from the wound and his breath hissed out the ragged hole. The smell filled my nostrils. I slammed the bloody, broken wood into him again and again.

My lungs sucked in air and I tasted his blood in my mouth. Expecting Joaquin's knifepoint between my ribs, I spun toward the stairs. The Spaniard lay in a lifeless heap against the end of the bar. Flames sputtered from a dozen wet pools on the wood floor. June stood halfway down the staircase. Shards of broken glass lay all around her bare feet. Her fingers clenched the banister.

"He hurt Miss May." Her words floated out, like from a trance. "They was gonna kill us all."

She stared down at Joaquin's burnt coat and face. "I hit him with that coal-oil lamp." Her fingers found the ends of a strand of hair and began to twist it. Her head tilted like a puppy dog. "Did I kill him?"

"What the–?" Sheriff Beard burst through the door.

"More blood than a slaughterhouse in here." He nudged Madison with the end of his axe handle, then looked up at me and shook his head.

He crouched down next to Jonesy. "He's breathin' but his skull's cracked for sure."

May pulled herself to her knees, caught hold of the edge of a table and struggled to her feet.

"Kepler saved us all," she said. She caught the edge of her dress and wiped it across her mouth. She limped toward the bar and stamped out the last burning puddle of coal oil. She paused an instant at Joaquin's body, then spit blood on his corpse. She snapped up a bottle of whiskey from behind the bar and tipped the bottle to her mouth.

"Madison asked for it, he did," she said, wiping the whiskey from her chin. "Kepler just did what he had to. Now, Sheriff, get this other trash outta my place." She took another long drink from the bottle and turned her back to me.

June's cat slipped in from behind the bar and padded up the staircase. She bent down and caught the cat up in her arms. She touched her lips to the top of Mister Bugg's head and began to sing.

Beard grabbed my arm and pulled me outside. "Some fellas from the railroad found me and told me Madison and his cutthroats came in looking for trouble. I got here as fast as I could. The way I see it, you did what needed done. Less'n someone tells me different, I'm calling it self-defense."

He leaned on his axe handle. "Ain't too many people in this town gonna cry over losin' this bunch." He pointed at the hole in my sleeve. "You shot?"

"I don't think so." My arm stung but the rest of me felt

nothing. When I touched my arm, I felt the burnt tear in the coat.

"Don't appear to be bleedin'. Now git to your room like you promised me. Rest up and come by the office in the mornin'."

Beard went back inside.

My knees trembled. There was no comfort on the dark street. When my tongue touched my lips, I tasted the death that clung to me. The sleep I needed wouldn't come tonight. Too many dead men would visit my dreams.

I peeled off my stained coat and dropped it on a smoldering ash pile in the alley behind my hotel. I climbed the back stairs to my room on the second floor. In the dark hall, I fumbled in my pockets for the key and stabbed it into the lock.

Silvery threads of a broken spider web floated in the breeze through the open window. I struck a match and lit the candle on my bureau. For a long minute, I stared at my face in the mirror. I'd had a ticket to Denver in my hand last night. A chance to flee all this, but I had stayed. And now I'd killed a man.

I filled the basin with water, slipped out of my shirt and dabbed the gash on my bicep where Madison's bullet had grazed my arm. My teeth ground together as rough cloth touched raw flesh, but I was happy for the pain. It reassured me that I was still alive.

The floor squeaked behind me. From the shadowy corner of my dark room, a voice spoke.

"Kepler, I need your help." It was Landry.

I whirled around. My hip jostled the chest of drawers and the water pitcher and basin shattered on the floor around my feet. The candle's flame quivered in the cold breeze. Then all went dark.

I sensed Landry stand up near the old chair in the corner. Slowly, my eyes changed the blackness to shades of charcoal and gray. Her white teeth flashed in the night. When I found her eyes, it was as if the light from the farthest star reflected back at me in a purple tinge of color.

My hip pushed against the drawer handles and I eased my hand toward the small pistol tucked in my belt.

"Please, Kepler, I didn't mean to startle you. It's just that you are the only one who knows. You saw us in the forest. You know what he's done to me."

"How did you get in?"

"I came through the window. One of the advantages of this curse is the strength it allows me."

My heart raced but her words were calm. Without moving my eyes from the sound of her voice I fumbled on the bureau for my matches to relight the candle.

"Please don't."

Though she'd had the opportunity, she'd made no move to harm me. Did she not want me to see her? Was she caught somewhere between the human shape and that of the wolf? Perhaps the light might give me some small advantage.

I snapped the match head on the table's corner and my other hand slid to the gun from my behind my hip. The smell of burning sulfur filled the air.

"Not the candle, please." In the orange halo, Landry snatched the blankets from my bed and draped them over her naked body. "Use the oil lamp."

The match's flame touched my fingertips and I dropped

it. My hand found the pistol. I trained its muzzle towards the shadowy corner of the room.

"Please, listen to me," she said through the blackness.

"I'll listen." I shifted the gun to my right hand.

"Nicolae wants to leave Colorado," Landry began. "It might be my only chance to get away from him. He decided that the Arizona Territory is more fitting. He has friends there."

"What has this to do with me?"

"Please." The blankets shifted on her skin. "Put the gun down."

"You can see me in the dark?" I tried to keep my voice even.

"Another advantage of this curse."

"I'm going to light the lamp. I need to see who I'm talking to." I turned, put the gun down and felt for the matchbox. Many times, I had bluffed my way at a poker table. I needed to show her that I wasn't afraid. But the hair stood on the back of my neck and images of bodies torn by animal fangs flooded my brain.

I lifted the glass on the oil lamp, touched the match to the wick and eased the globe back in place. Soft light spread over the room. Landry wrapped herself in the blankets from my bed. She gathered them in one hand so that they barely covered her breasts. Despite the cold, a sheen of perspiration shined on her shoulders.

"Go on," I said.

"You can't tell anyone what you saw."

"What makes you think I haven't already?"

"You have no proof. Say anything and you'll be laughed at. You're smart enough to know that your credibility is all you have. Lose that and you'll never find another newspaper job."

My tongue stuck to the top of my mouth. I swallowed and tried to speak.

Landry brushed back her hair with one hand. "I must escape from him. His hunger grows stronger each day."

"How will I know that I won't end up like your friend, Tobias?"

"Tobias was a fool. He thought he could be one of us. Nicolae toyed with him." A hint of amusement lifted in her voice. "I don't think you're a fool, Mr. Kepler."

"Where is Nicolae now?"

"Not until I'm sure you'll help me." Her head tilted forward and her eyes turned to purple flames. I thought of the wolf that I had seen tear the life from Oscar on the riverbank. And how that same animal had stalked the edge of the river, wanting to come for me.

"How am I to know this isn't some kind of trick?" I moved my fingers toward my gun. "And if I help, what's in it for me?"

She stood from the chair, still clutching the blanket around her body, and turned her back toward me. "No matter what you saw in the forest, you'll never understand." The blanket fell away from her naked skin. "Look at me!"

I pressed back against the wall. She was gaunt. Skin, pulled tight over her ribs, shined in the faint light. Muscle and sinew flexed beneath her flesh. Dark red scratch marks raked her back and hips. Shame made me want to turn away, but I couldn't.

"Look," she demanded.

A line of coarse, dark hair traced the center of her neck and ran down her spine. The alabaster skin I remembered from the first time I had seen her in Nicolae's train car was now mottled and scaly.

"I was fifteen when he found me." She looked at me over her naked shoulder. "My parents both died when the cholera spread through the city. The only way I could live was to sell myself." I saw tears pool in her eyes. "He found me in the cribs and promised to care for me. At first it was all he said it would be. We left San Francisco and traveled. New places. Clothes, food, wine."

Her voice quivered. "His special red wine. He made me drink it. All those weeks I drank his wine."

She pulled the blanket back to her shoulders and turned to face me. The lamp hissed for fuel and the flame dimmed.

"One night he came to my room. I was drunk from his wine."

A tear left the corner of her eye, slipped down the side of her nose until it pooled in the shadowy line of soft black hair above her lip. Her mouth twisted.

"I thought it would be like the other times," she continued. "I knew there was a price for all he gave me. But the color of his eyes was different that night and right before, he–changed." She lowered her face. "The animal took me," she whispered.

Landry pulled the blanket from her chest. "See his marks on me."

My breath caught in my throat. Her fingers touched a shiny scar above her left breast. The wound glistened in the lamplight. Faint dark hair, like on her back, made a column from her breasts to the thatch between her legs.

She saw my stare, covered herself and sank onto the chair. My legs went weak and I clung to the bureau to keep from falling. Landry hung her head and spoke slowly.

"For the next few days I was racked with a fever and drifted in and out of sleep. When I began to recover, it was like my blood burned in my veins. I needed red meat and Nicolae's wine. Little by little I regained my strength and he taught me to hunt." She peeked up at me from beneath her dark hair. "Hunt men." Her tongue swept over her lips.

Everything I knew about this earth and the heavens over it turned to doubt. The torn bodies, the wolves that became humans, all the nightmares I ignored to fill my money belt took the form of this creature before me. All the more, did she want my help, or was this part of their scheme to use me? Even the pistol at my fingertips gave no comfort.

Strands of spittle clung to her teeth. "My first kill was here. I was clumsy. I broke a woman's neck like he had trained me, but I had no stomach to feed. Nicolae had killed a man the night before and did not need her blood. He hung the woman in a tree by the river."

And I had found her body my first day in Brokeheart.

I summoned a bit of courage. "What do you want from me?"

"Keep our secret," she pleaded. "I must get back before he misses me. I'll come to you again."

She climbed from the chair leaving the blanket. My stomach churned at her strange beauty and horrible marks.

Her hand reached toward me. The curved tip of her fingernail found the wound on my arm. She dabbed at my seeping blood and then touched the finger to her tongue.

The place she touched me turned to fire.

With that, she caught the window sash and pulled it open. She stepped onto the roof, dropped to her hands and knees and crawled to the roof's edge. Landry turned and looked back at me. "I'll come to you again," she whispered and then dropped like a cat to the alley below.

I fell to my knees at the window and watched her disappear into the darkness.

Vivid dreams tormented my sleep. I told myself over and over that none of it was true, that when morning came everything would be different, that I had not killed a man. Men in the form of wolves did not stalk the night. And Landry would never return. Only that would ransom me from my doubts. Two nights without rest finally took hold and I surrendered into some semblance of sleep.

When I awoke, it was nearly nine o'clock the next morning. Six inches of new snow covered the streets and rooftops of Brokeheart. I dressed and went downstairs.

The clerk behind the front desk called to me, "Good to see you back, Kepler." He dipped a quill in the inkwell and studied the ledger spread on the desktop. "Best be careful," he clucked. "That old man who brings the firewood claims he found wolf tracks in the mud out in the alley this morning. Just a stray dog, I'd reckon."

Chapter Sixteen

The publisher of the *Brokeheart Gazette* perched half of his massive rear end on the edge of my desk. Dust swirled in the gentle afternoon light as Wilson huffed out a breath of stale air.

"Kepler, what's got into you?" he asked. "It's nearly four weeks since you came back here from Leadville. You haven't given me one decent story. I'm a tolerant man, but I need something to print." He pulled off his glasses and pinched the bridge of his nose. "All this with Madison made you some kind of hero 'round here. He cut corners and stole. Each day they're uncoverin' somethin' else he did. People in this town figure you did 'em a favor."

He laid the slab of his hand on my shoulder. "You've nothing to be ashamed of. Magistrate cleared you of all wrongdoin's last week. People want to hear from you again. And I need you, too."

I tilted back in my chair and found a fly speck on the ceiling to stare at. I chewed on my lower lip and bit down until it hurt. I knew he was right.

After a long moment, I spoke. "It's more than Madison. A lot of things have cluttered my mind."

"You thinkin' of movin' on?"

"I'm just not sure."

"I could make demands, you know."

"No." I shook my head and looked him in the eye.

"You took a chance on me when I needed it. I owe you that much."

Wilson pushed his glasses back between his wooly eyebrows. "What say you introduce yourself to that new superintendent at the mine? See what he has to say 'bout all the new goin's on. There's a rumor 'bout expansion. He's heard 'bout you, no doubt."

"And if he volunteers anything about Madison's . . ."

The corners of Wilson's mouth turned up under his mustache. "Could make for good readin, if'n he would."

From across the river, the mine whistle sounded. Wilson tugged his watch from his vest pocket, held it at arm's length and peered over his glasses. "Five o'clock on the button. Quittin' time. Might be a good time to catch the new superintendent." He lifted himself up from my desk. "His name's Steele. Horace Steele."

Wilson lumbered toward the door. "Oh," he said. "Package came in from the San Francisco newspaper this afternoon. Got your name on it. That where you're applyin' for a job?"

"No, sir. I asked a friend to send me some back issues for a matter I'm researching." I stood up from my desk and took my coat from the antlers tacked to the wall.

"Story in it?"

"Perhaps."

I touched the place where the bullet had grazed my arm before I slid my hand into the coat sleeve.

"That arm still botherin' you?" Wilson asked. "You best have old Doc Stone have a look at that. Shoulda healed up by now."

A fresh layer of whitewash had been splashed on the miners' shacks. A little boy tugged at his mother's skirt and pointed at me. She scooped the boy into her arms and smiled as I passed by. A line of workers, still in their muddy overalls, tipped their hats and stepped out of my way.

I found Horace Steele in the office building. He sat at a rolltop desk paging through a pile of receipts. His pale eyes brightened when I introduced myself.

"Forgive me for not seeking you out earlier," he said as I took his firm handshake. "Your name has come up more than once since I arrived here."

"I'm not sure what to say."

"I don't believe anything needs to be said. My wife—she's still in Denver—makes it a point to read everything you've written. She'll be pleased to find my name in one of your articles. In fact, she sent this," he fumbled in the clutter on his desk. "Came in the mail just yesterday. Did you know you're in *Harper's Magazine*?"

He wet his thumb on his tongue and flipped through several pages in the magazine, then handed it to me.

In bold letters the title read, "Crusading Reporter Kills Cruel Mine Owner." Smaller letters above a crude ink drawing said, "A Vicious Gunfight." The drawing showed a bearded man, meant to be an image of Simon Lagree, clutching his chest with one hand while a pistol fell from the other. A smoking gun pointed from the hand of a clean-shaven, handsome fellow in a white Stetson.

"About the only part they got right is how good-looking I am," I said.

Steele laughed and offered me a chair. "Now what is it I can do for you?"

"Are you replacing Madison?" I sat down.

"Only temporarily. I'm here to assess what needs to be done to get this mine back to a profitable state. Madison ran this like his own fiefdom. Management's fault."

"So the rumors are true?"

"Yes."

Full dark filled the windows by the time Steele finished explaining the dangerous shortcuts Madison had allowed in the construction of the mine tunnels, unaccounted-for expenditures, and missing equipment. He slammed shut a payroll ledger and added, "People respect you, Kepler. I'm giving you full permission to explain what I've laid out here. If you'll come back on Friday, an accountant from the main office will share the specifics. Can you wait until then?"

"I'll discuss it with my editor but I don't see any reason why he won't agree."

"Fine, then you will have the information before any of the papers in Denver." He leaned back on his chair and laced his fingers together behind his head.

"One more thing," I asked. "I need to speak with one of your employees. An Indian. Joe Medicine Pony. I heard Madison hired him."

"I think I know the name." Steele said. "He's stringing timbers in the number four shaft."

The wall lamp sputtered and then faded to a red glow. Streaks of light snaked down the hall outside my hotel room. I sucked in a deep breath and put the key in the lock. Would Landry be waiting inside?

Darkness blended with shadows cast by moonlight. Old floorboards creaked under my feet. I pulled the door shut and, like I did every night, searched the dark corners for any movement. Like the presses at the *Gazette* forced ink on paper, everything about the night she visited—every word, every sight, even her touch on my arm—was printed on my memory. A part of me longed to see her again.

In the glow of the coal-oil lamp, my pen toyed on the paper. Wilson expected something soon, but the bundle from San Francisco held my attention. I gave up on the promised story, tore open the package and leafed through the worn paper.

By midnight I had read the pages and separated the stack into two piles. The first contained articles on cholera epidemics and when they had occurred. The next, deaths caused by wild animals.

I drifted to sleep confused by the first pile and frightened by the second.

Chapter Seventeen

I found Joe Medicine Pony before the work whistle blew the next morning. The other miners shifted from foot to foot in the cold air. They balanced shovels, pry bars, and sledge hammers on their shoulders, ready to go underground for the day's work. The miners' breath mingled in a steamy cloud above their muted conversations.

Joe stepped away from the group. He pinched a bit of the pollen from the leather pouch he carried around his neck. With a flick of his wrist the yellow dust swirled away in the breeze from the creek bottom. Joe raised his open palms to the sky and tilted his head back. The new sun washed over his craggy brown skin. I waited until his eyes opened and then pushed through the group of workers.

"Joe?"

He turned his weathered face.

"I need to talk to you," I whispered. "Remember how you told me there was evil in this town? That the man in the train car changed the harmony?"

Joe's face showed no expression.

"I need to know more. When can we talk?"

The steam whistle sounded. The men around us ambled toward the mine entrance. Joe's black eyes studied his boot tops.

"Evil still here," he said without raising his face. He turned and fell into line with the others.

"Joe," I called out.

He glanced back. His fingers touched the pouch at his neck and then he walked into the black mine entrance.

The little boy I recognized from the day before waved at the disappearing line of men. The boy slashed at the soft earth beside a mud puddle with a sharpened willow stick. A dark-haired girl took his hand. They both smiled when they saw me. Neither wore coats.

"You're Kepler? The one that killed Madison?" the girl asked.

The boy hid behind her worn skirt. He rose on his toes and peeked over her shoulder.

"That's me." I dropped on one knee and looked at the girl's face. "It's nothing I'm proud of."

"Papa said you did a good thing. He was a bad man. Madison, I mean." She caught a strand of hair that stuck to the corner of her mouth and pushed it away.

"It's never good when someone dies. No matter how bad we think he is."

"Alls I know is that when Madison went away, my Papa was happy. Mama's more happy now, too." She tugged her dress away from the boy's fingers. "We got brand new paint on our house. There's more food now. Firewood, too. That new man says they're gonna build us a school." The girl pulled her brother's arm and he stepped beside her. "Mama's worried about Papa, though. She don't like him doin' that work down in the mine. She says he goes down deep in the ground. I hear her cryin' sometimes at night."

"Your Mama take you into town?"

"Sometimes. More since you killed Madison. She says we're goin' today. Gonna buy me some new shoes. Real new ones that nobody wore 'fore me."

I winked at her. "Tell you what. You know the man that runs the big store on Front Street?"

"Man with the gray beard?"

"Tell him I sent you. He'll have a piece of candy for each of you. Just tell me your names."

The girl beamed. "Ain't had candy since last Christmas. I'm Mary. This here's my brother Paulie."

"Not Paulie." The little boy pushed in front of his sister. He held up his stick and clasped it with both hands in front of his face, then with all the seriousness of a judge, said, "I'm *Paul* Novatni."

"Well, Paul Novatni, tell the man at the store I sent you."

Paul pulled away from his sister and scraped his stick across the wet ground. He raked the sharp tip over a clover-shaped depression in the mud. The track of a wolf. Landry had left a similar mark in the mud behind my hotel. My stomach turned sour.

A scrawny dog scampered up. Muddy paws batted at Paul's pants. He pushed the dog away.

My stomach righted itself. Dog tracks. *Just the tracks of a cur dog*, I told myself.

I tried the door of the store on Front Street and found it still locked. I tapped on the window. The shopkeeper opened the door.

"I should have been open by now." The bearded man fumbled with his coat. "A big coyote tore hell out of the family dog. I had to shoot the poor animal. Wife and kids are still bawling. I think they loved that dog more than me."

I asked him how much the best pair of children's shoes

would cost and then handed him enough to buy a pair for a boy and a girl with a nickel extra for candy. I told him the Novatnis would be in sometime that day.

Two loaded freight wagons with teams of eight plodded down Front Street. Cutting between the wagons, I hurried past the Chinaman's and jumped up on the boardwalks on Main.

A bank clerk turned the key in the lock of the front door and opened for the day. I was the first customer.

Owens, the bank manager, recognized me and waved for me to come into his office. "I must again tell you how sorry we are you felt the need to transfer your funds to that bank in Cheyenne." Owens was a pinch-faced man. I thought of lemons every time I spoke with him.

"Business opportunity, that's all," I told him. "Now what do we need to look over this morning?"

"Your approval is needed to release monies for the construction crew's payroll." An envelope with my name printed on the front sat at the center of his tidy desk. He pushed it toward me.

"Let me review this." I picked up the papers. "Can you give me a few minutes alone? If everything is in order I'll give my okay." I enjoyed the sneer on his face when I said the word "alone." The manager got up to leave me. "Another thing, Owens. Could you check on the balance in my personal account?"

The report from Rosie outlined the progress that had been made on Nicolae's lodge. Windows and doors had been hung. He had released all the crew except for eight carpenters. Rosie finished the summary by saying he planned on being done in time to earn his bonus. A flourish in his signature made me sure things on the mountain were going smoothly.

I stared a long moment at the paper. Landry had told me Nicolae was planning on leaving for the Arizona Territory. Considering the money he had invested in the lodge, I didn't see him abandoning it. I signed the paper. I wanted to be sure Rosie and his men were paid at once.

Owens's feet paced by the door, turned and crossed back to where they started. After he had made two more trips, I called for him. I handed him the papers and told him to expedite the workers' paychecks.

"Kepler, your account has a balance of twelve hundred dollars. It seems the weekly stipend from Mr. Nicolae has doubled."

I bit down on my lip to hide my surprise.

My plans had been to spend what was left of the morning at the *Gazette* trying to compose the promised article for Wilson. But this news of Nicolae's generosity, the Indian's unwillingness to talk, and my confused thoughts concerning Landry twisted back and forth in my brain. I decided a long ride on Seer might give me time to sort through my thoughts.

Three long shrieks of the mine whistle changed all that.

Shop doors all along Main Street flung open. Owens and his clerks spilled onto the boardwalk in front of the bank. The Chinaman wiped his hands on his stained apron and peered toward where the sound came from. Three more blasts cut through the air. I ran from Main Street back to the mine.

A cloud of dust, as fine as sifted flour, belched out of the mine entrance. A miner burst through the blur. He stumbled to his knees, hacking and coughing. Two more followed. Then another. Men raced to pull them away from the mass of suspended grit still spilling from the entrance.

Off to one side, a dozen miners coated in dirt sprawled on the ground. Their chests heaved for breath. Children and women from the shacks near the creek crowded around the group.

A round, white-haired woman pulled free of another's arms. She pushed her way into the cluster of men, fell on her knees beside one man and wrapped her arms around his neck. The man grabbed her face and pressed his dust-coated lips to hers.

Mary Novatni folded her skinny arms tight around her little body. Paul clung to his mother's skirt. One balled fist pressed tight against the woman's mouth. Tears cut streaks through the dirt that clung to her face.

Sheriff Beard elbowed his way through the gathering crowd of townsfolk. He tipped his head for me to follow. Steele and three of his foremen studied a chart they had spread over a pile of rough-cut timbers.

"What do you know so far?" Beard asked as we walked up.

Steele ran his fingers through his hair. He let out a deep breath and then pointed at the diagram. "We think it happened right here. A team was replacing timbers in the number four shaft, roof came down on 'em. Thank God we were able to seal it off before that dust cloud rolled through the whole mine."

"Anybody still in there?" I asked.

"Not sure. We're counting now. No sign of a driller in shaft three. We haven't found the Indian yet." Steele rubbed his mouth. "And the lead man's still missin'."

"What's his name?"

"Novatni."

I looked back at the women and children. Mary leaned on her mother's shoulder. Paul still held tight to her skirt.

"It's all Madison's fault," Steele stammered. "He okayed the lumber used in that shaft. That's why I've had a crew in there every day this week." He grabbed one of his workers by the front of his shirt. "Count 'em. Then count again. I want to know who's out and who's left inside." He pushed the man away.

Steele turned to his next manager. "Get some men together and build some fires. I want the families warm. I know that they won't leave until they know everyone is safe. Have some food sent from town. Do it, now." The foreman hustled away.

"Sheriff, if you could bring the priest, I know it would be a comfort for these people." Steele rubbed his hands together and then looked up into the sky. Snowflakes the size of burro's hooves began to fall. "We'll need every prayer he can say."

Steele looked at me. "Kepler, these people respect you. They don't know me from Adam. I want you to stay close. I might need you to talk to them. This is Will Stevenson." He nodded to a round-shouldered man bent over a chart. "My mining engineer. He knows more about underground mining than I ever will. He's going to tell me what needs to be done to get those men out of there. Kepler, you'll tell those families what our plans are. I'll pay you for it. Out of my own pocket, if need be."

"I don't need your money."

Stevenson flicked the snow off the map. "From what I see here, if they're behind the cave-in, they'll have air. But if it took out the pumps, that shaft will fill with water. I need to take this inside where I can study it."

"Go ahead, then. I'll stay with these people." Steele buttoned his coat and turned up the collar. "Walk with me, Kepler."

Bonfires came to life. Women and their children huddled close together. Miners hauled wood. People returned to their shacks and came back with blankets and coats. Townsfolk drifted back to their shops and homes. Father Dowd moved between the fires, touching shoulders and making the sign of the cross.

The Novatni family found a place at the fire closest to the mine entrance. They sat with their backs to the flames, watching for any hint of promise to emerge from the black pit.

By mid-afternoon, the sky turned the color of gray steel. Snow came in squalls, and the flakes that made it to the ground melted into the trampled ooze. A wagonload of miners who escaped through another entrance joined waiting families.

Candles burned in a makeshift shrine thrown up with lumber and covered with canvas. An old woman brought a crucifix from the wall of her shack and placed it among the flickering lights. As miners emerged from the hole, Father Dowd pinched out candles until only three burned.

Horace Steele brushed the snowflakes from his shoulders. "Ever been at a cave-in before?"

Before I could answer, he continued.

"This is my third. My first job. Twenty-two years ago. Pennsylvania coal mine. Lost eleven men. I still hear the families cryin' for those they lost. Vowed I'd never let that happen again while I was in charge." Steele tugged at his coat collar. "Two years ago, near Georgetown. Roof came down on a team repairing track. Three got out, three more trapped. It took us the best part of two days, but we got to them. I'll do whatever it takes."

A buckboard clattered over the bridge. Sheriff Beard smacked the ends of the reins on the horses' flanks. The team strained into their harness and climbed the slick gravel road. As the wagon rolled to a stop, May eased off the seat beside the sheriff and hurried to the back. Steam from two great kettles swirled up, mingling with the falling snow. June tossed a blanket off her head and face and climbed off of the buckboard. The two women wrestled one of the pots to the back of the wagon. May snatched up a ladle and stirred the big pot. In just minutes, a line of dirty men and women curled up to the wagon. June handed out bread and May filled the plates. Miners and their wives dipped their heads as they passed. Children smiled up at the two women and followed their parents back to the fires.

The sheriff walked to where Steele and I were standing, carrying full plates.

"Seemed everybody wanted to know who was payin' for the food 'ceptin' May." The sheriff handed the food to Steele and me. "She heard what happened. One of hers had traded for a hind quarter of elk. She set that black gal to makin' a stew. Chinaman sent the bread."

"May's the woman with the saloon there on Front Street?" Steele asked as he mopped the bread through his stew. "I'll see to it she's paid."

"Don't think she's rightly concerned 'bout that."

Beard turned and looked over the muddy scene. The

Novatnis hadn't left their place by the fire nearest the main entrance. With Paul at one shoulder and Mary at the other, the woman sat like a small monument of hope. June bent forward and gave each of the children a plate of the elk stew. She set a plate on the woman's lap, but the mother's arms never moved from her children. June peeled the blanket from her own shoulders and draped it over the woman's back and hair. Paul dipped his fingers in the stew, and Mary lifted her face to smile at June.

"Her man still in there?" June sloshed to where we stood. Mud was splattered along the hem of her red dress and on her bare legs. Her feet were wrapped in strips of burlap, now soaked with the mire. She pulled her lips tight along her teeth to fight off the chill. I shucked off my coat and hung it around her tiny shoulders. She leaned her head against my side and I felt her weariness rush into me.

"We can't account for her husband and two others. One is the Indian, Joe. You know him?" I asked her.

"May'd have me sneak 'im a whiskey out the back. She liked him enough, but wouldn't let no Indian in the front door." June looked up at Steele. "They dead?"

"We just don't know, young lady," Steele said.

June tilted her head. "Sir, you're the first one ever call me a lady." She pulled off my coat and gave it back to me. "Gots to get back to help May. Another blanket in the wagon there."

June's rag boots slopped through the mud. She paused at the little memorial with the three candles. She looked back at the Novatnis, bowed her head, and squished her eyes shut. Her lips moved and I had no doubt what she prayed for.

"Damn, damn, damn," Steele breathed out the words. "Where's Stevenson?"

"He's checkin' the pumps," a worker said.

"Get him up here." A snowflake caught on his mustache and melted away. "Get him, now."

Sheriff Beard, Steele, and I looked at the map the mining engineer spread over an empty barrel top. He drew a pencil stub across the paper. "Pumps are still pullin' water. That's the good news. The bad part is they're drawing only half of what they should be. Could mean anything. Damaged pipe. Maybe the cave-in clogged the shaft and there's not as much water comin' in. Just don't know."

He pointed with the pencil. "Right here. Novatni's crew said that when the timber broke, they saw the Indian grab him and pull him back. The dirt came down and the crew hightailed it out. If the Indian got 'im free of the cave-in they'd be about here." He tapped the paper.

"What about the third man?" The mist from Steele's breath washed over the chart.

"No word on him at all 'cept for some crazy talk about about hearin' a wolf howl before the roof gave way." Stevenson shook his head. "Means nothing. Sound of a cave in'll make the bravest deep-pit man wet himself."

I jerked my head around, trying to spy the paw print in the mud Paul Novatni had poked with his stick. Muddy feet from all those waiting miners and families had churned away any sign of it. I thought that a kid's dog had left the mark. But maybe it was Nicolae and Landry's warning for me. I bit down on my lip to battle the tremor that chilled my spine.

"Is there any way to get to those two?" Steele's fist pounded the barrel top.

"Maybe." Stevenson looked each of us in the eye and then pointed to the chart. "Here. Map shows an airshaft that comes down, splits and ends up maybe twenty yards from where I think the roof came down." He looked up at Steele.

"Just what does that mean?"

"If we can trust this map—Madison took a lotta short-cuts—it means they got air. And it might mean we got a way to get 'em."

"Go on."

"It's a slim chance, but it's all I know." Stevenson tucked the pencil behind his ear. "A hundred feet straight down from the top to where the airshaft splits. The leg we need angles down to where I think they might be. Maybe another couple hundred feet. The map shows the main shaft to be a three-foot square." He motioned with his hands. "I asked some of the miners 'bout it. They don't think it's that big. We just might be able to lower a man down the main shaft and he could belly crawl down this angle. I got no idea how big or just how steep that tunnel is. If he makes it, and if they're still alive, we'd could decide whether to pull 'em out the way he went in. Or repair the cave-in and get to 'em."

"Any other way?" Steele leaned close.

"Only to repair the tunnel. That could take days."

"Just where is this airshaft?"

"'Bout two miles up that hill. There's a wagon trail." Stevenson looked up at the sky. "If we're gonna get there, we need to go now. Before the snow's too deep."

Steele shook his head. "How are you going to get a man to the bottom of the shaft?"

"Railroad's got a winch with three hundred feet of half-inch cable. We can lower him down with that."

"We'll try it." Steele locked his eyes on his engineer. "I don't want to create any false hope. Keep this quiet until we know something. Now who's going down there?"

"I'll do it," Beard said.

"No." Steele rubbed his hand over his face. "I'll ask one of my foremen to volunteer."

Beard raised a hand. "If you're gonna keep it quiet it's gotta be one of us four."

"But with your size, you'll never fit down that shaft." I looked through the window at the Novatnis. "I'll go. Besides, there might be a story at the bottom." *Or a pair of wolves.*

Stevenson jumped on the back of the buckboard and the sheriff skidded the wagon through the mud into town. While the two of them loaded the winch in the wagon, I bought lanterns, coal oil, gloves, and a length of rope at the general store.

Two faint depressions in the snow marked the road up the hillside. Beard clucked at the team and urged them up the hill. Powdery snow covered the ruts. Shadows from the trees forced the cold air down my collar and through each buttonhole in my coat. Stevenson watched his map as best he could and looked for any landmarks to tell us how far we'd gone.

We climbed through the pine forest until we broke out in a snow-covered meadow. At the far edge, the snow heaped up over a mound of what Stevenson guessed was the tailings left from digging the airshaft.

"Let's get things set up." Stevenson folded the map and tucked it away.

It was just a black hole—blacker than black against the pure white snow. Beard found a peach-sized rock in the bed of the buckboard and pitched into the shaft. It rattled off the sides. I strained but never heard it hit bottom. Didn't matter. I was going down.

We tied the winch off to a twisted spruce as big as a man's waist and played the cable out to the edge of the hole. Beard flipped a timber across the opening, rigged a pulley to the middle of the log and passed the end of the cable through the sheave.

"I thought this over," Stevenson double-checked the line. "We'll tie one of those lanterns to maybe ten foot of rope. Hang that off the end of the cable. We'll tie you in above it. That way you'll have some light as you go down. When you get to the bottom, leave the lantern there. It'll give a reference point as you crawl that side shaft. Take these." He handed me a half-dozen candles as big around as half dollars. "Each one will burn about an hour. Use them as you crawl. And here's a box of matches. I wrapped it in oilcloth to keep them dry."

Stevenson took the rope and wove a harness around my waist and hips. "It's gonna get damp, maybe real wet in the side shaft. Deeper you go the warmer it'll be. We'll freeze our butts off up here, but you'll be warm." He forced a smile. "And Kepler, we'll wait. We won't leave you."

I slipped out of my jacket and stuffed the package of candles and matches inside my shirt. Sheriff Beard handed me a pair of gloves. He turned his shoulders and face, then spun back. Beard clamped his hand on my shoulder and bowed his head.

"Say a good one, preacher," Stevenson said.

I straddled the opening and my weight settled into the harness. On a strip of bare dirt, next to the toe of my boot, the distinct impression of a wolf track pressed into the earth. Before Beard said his "amen" I smudged out the footprint with the sole of my boot.

Beard looked me in the eye. I faked a shiver and nodded down the airshaft. "He promised me it would be warmer down there."

Stevenson lit the lantern and lowered it into the hole. I slipped over the log, and when Beard lifted his hand, I let my weight drop into the ropes. It cut into the skin around my waist and bit through my pants into my thighs. Beard turned the winch handle and with a jolt each time the teeth of the ratchet caught, I dropped into the mine an inch at a time.

I kicked loose a cloudburst of gravel that pinged off the lantern and jangled down into the darkness of the shaft. The rough walls rubbed my elbows and shoulders. With each click of the winch the sides tapered in. My body blocked all the lantern's light except orange slivers that sliced up. Above my head, the gray skies faded to a dot, then died away. The darkness tightened like the tunnel walls. I forced myself to breathe in small, even breaths, afraid a deep one would wedge me in this pit forever.

With the next few jerks of the cable, the passageway opened. My shoulders scraped away from the sides. Yellow light swept up. I heard the lantern touch the bottom. With one more turn of the handle, it tumbled over and sputtered. My eyes clamped shut, sure the lantern would rupture and

I would be lowered into its flaming oil. Warm air gushed up all around me, so warm I trembled.

The tips of my toes scraped the gravelly floor. Then my boot soles touched. Two more turns of the winch handle and I was standing. I crouched and grabbed the lantern bail and set it upright. It hissed for fuel, popped, and the light brightened.

I had to stoop in the dome-shaped space. A bitter muskiness filled the chamber. Liquid drizzled off the stone walls and formed wet marks on the floor. I touched the pool with my fingers and lifted them to my nose. The odor of animal urine gagged me. The wolves had marked their presence in the mine.

I wanted to tug on the cable and scream for Beard to pull me from the hellish pit. Instead, I stripped off the stained glove and tossed it away.

Two tunnels fed into the room. The warm air rushed up from my right—the one Stevenson said would lead to Novatni and the Indian. If I waited, I knew I might not go further. I dropped onto my knees and fumbled for one of the candles. When I lit it, the current of warm air blew it out. Three times I tried. Each time the ghostly breeze snuffed the flame.

I bit down on my lip and wriggled into the dark opening. Only by pushing my arms out in front on me, clawing at the rocks and pushing with the toes of my boots could I move forward. The darkness turned thick. Sweat from the hot air and my own exertion streamed into my eyes. I pushed forward for six breaths and then rested, then six more. Wet gravel soaked my shirt. The smell of the wolf's urine hung so thick I could taste it. And still I pushed forward.

Since I left my mother in Kansas City, I had clawed with fingernails and boot toes to the next adventure, the next job, the next woman, the next dollar. Finally the cards fell my way in Brokeheart. People knew my name. I had more money in the bank than I ever thought I'd see at one time. But I had nothing. Novatni had a wife and children waiting, hoping and praying for him. If I died in this hole, the stable would sell Seer and my saddle. Perhaps June would lay some flowers on the hillside. In a few months I'd be forgotten.

It wasn't the chance at a story that had brought me here. It wasn't the tears on Novatni's wife's face. I was here for me. The Indian told me about the evil that hung over the town. I had seen that evil in slaughtered bodies and in Nicolae, the man that became a wolf. Now this great sinfulness chose to harm the miners I had championed. Joe had a piece of the answer I sought.

I dug my nails into the blackness and inched forward.

The rocks I touched became June's shoulders. Landry's naked body lay just beyond my next handhold. Whiskey from the Months seeped from the tunnel sides.

Then a voice.

The slightest tremble above my own breathing.

I quieted every thought and willed all my strength to my ears. Again I heard it. With all I had, I dragged myself forward.

The angel whispered again.

"... my son, Paulie ..." So faint.

"Novatni!" I screamed. "Joe!"

My words came back in a thousand echoes. I gasped for breath to call again and the tunnel clamped rocky fingers around my chest. Panic wanted me. I sucked in the warm air and listened. Between the beats of my heart, I heard the voice again.

"Who?" the voice seeped back to me. "Where are you?"

I grabbed handfuls of the slick stones and pulled forward. In five body lengths, the top of the opening slipped off my shoulders. I lifted onto my hands and knees and sloshed through running water. "Novatni."

"Here."

Only a few feet from me.

The black darkness captured all. I could not see my hands touch the water I crawled in. I found the cave walls with the flats of my hands. My fingers followed the stone upward until I could stand.

"Where are you?" the voice called from the black.

"I'm going to light a candle." My fingers fumbled for the matches and struck one on the rock wall. The scratch exploded into a yellow flare. Its tendrils of light bored into the blackness. I touched the candle wick to the flame.

"Thank God. Are there others?" he called, slopping through the ankle-deep water.

"Are you Novatni?"

"Yes." He froze at the edge of the light's halo.

"Where did you . . . ? Are you alone?" he whispered.

I splashed towards him. "Where's the Indian?"

"Back there. He's hurt. But—"

I pressed the candle into his hand. "Listen to me." I lifted another candle to his. "I crawled down an airshaft. We can get you out. Your family is waiting. Tell me about Joe."

"I think his leg is broken," Novatni told me.

"Another man is missing."

"He's not with us." He shook his head.

"Take me to Joe." I had to see the Indian.

Novatni held the flickering candle above his head and led me through the passageway. Twice he stopped and held the light to the rock wall. His head tilted as he studied something.

In no more than a dozen yards, a pile of splintered timbers and rocks showed where the tunnel had collapsed. The Indian leaned against the side of the passageway. His head rested on his shoulder. Even in the pale candlelight, I could see the color had drained from his brown cheeks. His eyes barely opened as we sloshed up to where he lay.

"Joe." I knelt beside him. "It's me, Kepler. We're going to get you out of here."

He struggled to lift his head, and then it dropped onto his shoulder and his eyes shut.

"He's been like that the whole time," Novatni whispered. "Sometimes he's awake. Sometimes he sleeps."

Novatni moved his candle so I could look at Joe's legs. Dark red stained his overalls below his left knee.

"He saved my life," Novatni's low voice said. "He pulled me away from the cave-in. I heard him scream out. It was dark. I think a rock hit his leg. I tried to pull him away from here but it hurt him too much. I told him all about my family." He pointed in the shadows to a line of stones he'd arranged in the shape of a cross. "I prayed, too."

Water oozed from the mine's rocky walls. Joe's raspy breaths scraped off the ceiling and slipped down the passageway.

"How soon are they coming for us?" Novatni asked again.

I blew out my candle and took him by the shoulders. "The only chance was to send someone down the airshaft to see if you two were alive." I explained how I'd gotten to them. "You're going to crawl up the way I came. Your wife and children are waiting."

Novatni looked down at Joe.

"I'll stay with him," I said.

"You would do that?" Novatni wiped his fingers across his dirt-streaked face. "For him?" He nodded at the Indian.

"I have my reasons."

In the light of a single candle, I walked Novatni back to the airshaft that had brought me this far. I gave him another candle and half the matches. He started to speak, but I shook my head. He knelt and scrambled into the rocky passageway. I listened to him scrape over the gravel until the scratches faded away.

I slid down the wall and sat next to Joe. No color had returned to his pasty gray face. Stevenson told me that each candle would burn for an hour. I blew out the flame and rested against the rock wall. It made no difference if I closed my eyes or kept them open, the shades of blackness didn't change.

The love Novatni's family had for him would pull the tired miner up the shaft. I envied what he had. How long it would take them to come for Joe and me and just how they'd do it, I didn't know. In this dark pit, I'd have to wait and hope he'd regain consciousness. Maybe the shock of the injury would claim him first. Or wolves would sneak in through the darkness and kill us both.

Joe's ragged breath and the slow drip of water somewhere far down the tunnel were the only sounds. I counted each splash a hundred times. Then a thousand. Then a thousand more.

Fingers clutched my shirt sleeve, then fell away.

"Joe?"

I reached into the black. His hand grabbed my wrist. A soft moan cut the dark.

"Joe, stay still. I'll light a candle."

In the light, Joe pulled himself up onto one elbow. He winced as he fought to sit. "Water," he croaked softly.

"Let me see what I can find."

I lit another candle, left one beside Joe, and hurried down the tunnel toward the dripping sound. Just past the airshaft, the candlelight played over a dark liquid shine. A single sparkle dropped from the ceiling. It touched the shine and ripples rolled over its surface in slow circles.

I fell on my knees beside the puddle. Pebbles caught the candlelight and reflected back at me through the crystal clear water. I lifted up a handful and brought it to my lips. Its icy taste gave me new strength.

I needed a way to take some back to Joe. I tore a corner from the oilskin that wrapped the matches and rolled the few I had left in the scrap. I tugged off my boot, stuffed the remaining piece into the boot top and dipped the boot into the pool. Water poured from every seam but a bit stayed. It was hardly a mouthful. But it would have to do.

The dot of light from the candle I had left with Joe guided me back. I left my candle beside the small pond to show the way for the next trip. The Indian lapped the water from my boot and begged for more. Three times I returned to bring him what he needed.

Wax flowed from the half-burnt candle and covered the stones near Joe.

"Where Novatni?" he asked.

I explained what had happened and how Novatni was trying to climb to the surface.

"How long?" Joe rubbed his injured leg.

"I'm not sure," I said. "Even when he gets to the top, they'll have to decide how to get to us."

"You go back way you came."

"No, Joe. I'll wait with you."

He touched his dry lips. "Water?"

"Tell me something first." I blew out the candle. "Joe, what would turn a man into a wolf?"

Far down the tunnel, the point of light from the candle I left by the water shimmered. The next drop of water fell from the ceiling and plopped on the puddle. I curled my fingers around my wrist to count my pulse beats and waited for Joe to answer.

Tales for children. I don't believe in spirits, and I'm not so sure there's such a thing as evil.

I had spoken those words that first morning in Brokeheart. Now I needed some answers to my doubts, and I had risked my life to crawl into this pit to get them.

"Water," Joe whispered.

"Tell me about the evil."

Then all was quiet except for the drip on the water. We sat in the dark for a long time. Joe's breathing labored.

"The wisdomkeepers," Joe's voice was barely a whisper, "sent the evil ones into the belly of the mountain. To escape, they take shape of animals and hide among the—" He coughed. "Water, Kepler."

"As much as I can carry, just tell me a bit more."

"They have been with us since the beginning."

"Can they turn a human into one of them?"

"Evil ones find each other. When one, weak. More

together, very strong. Sometimes find man to help them. Feed like animals. Need man's blood."

Landry and Nicolae.

I looked down the shaft, expecting shadows to take the shape of wolves.

Joe babbled on. I picked out words like "moon" and "change" and "evil." I could hear his strength drain out of him. Finally, I reached out and touched his shoulder.

"Can they be killed?"

"Water?"

"How do you kill one?"

"Power from the earth. Much power. Fire. The metal from this mountain. White man's shiny metal." And with that, I heard him slump against the cavern wall.

"I'll get your water," I said to blackness. "As much as you can drink."

The candle at the pond burned away. I edged my way down the black tunnel by pressing my hands to the wall and counting steps to the puddle. I brought back water every few hours, or what I thought was hours. Joe drifted in and out of consciousness.

I slept, never sure whether it was for a few minutes or an entire day. Hunger twisted in my belly. My thoughts of what Joe's mumblings meant blended with dreams. Wolves stalked the black tunnels of this mountain. Blood seeped from the gravel where I sprawled. I'd jerk awake and count a hundred more splashes on the pond. I composed my own obituary in my mind. It disappointed me how little I'd really done.

Joe heard the sounds first. He groaned and in the dark I heard him struggle to sit up. I fumbled for the last match and tried to strike it. Its head peeled away on the rock wall.

The dampness in the mine soaked everything. Fighting tears I thought were used up, I tossed the stick away.

Then I heard it, too. Metal clanged on rock, faintly at first. A rhythm vibrated on the wall behind me and pushed back the silence. I felt my way toward the sound. Moist gravel clung to my palms. I touched the splintered timbers where the roof gave way.

I screamed my name. The sounds paused and then quickened.

"They're comin', Joe. They're comin' for us."

Chapter Eighteen

Sheriff Beard held my arm to keeping me from falling. White, hot sunshine from the mine entrance bored into the black. I lifted my arm to shield my eyes.

"How long was I . . . ?"

"It's near noon Thursday." The lawman wrapped his arm around my waist. "Like Jonah was three days and three nights in the belly of the great fish, you was three days and nights in the belly of this mountain."

"Did they find the third man?"

"Found him yesterday. Caught in the cave-in. Stones cut him up. If I didn't know better, I'd swear an animal tore him to pieces."

My knees buckled and the smell of wolf urine filled my nostrils. I told myself the smell was all in my head, that the muddy tracks were made by a kid's dog. Somewhere on the hills above the mine camp, a wolf howled. And my ears were the only ones that heard.

Beard jerked my arm over his shoulder and we stumbled the last few steps out of the mine. My eyes closed tightly in the sunlight. Someone hoisted my other arm over his shoulder. Around me I heard people clap their hands.

I turned to look over my shoulder and squinted. Steele held one side of a stretcher, Novatni the other. The Indian had been lashed to the litter. Stevenson carried the back by himself. The applause grew louder.

Steele raised his free hand. "I promised you we'd get 'em out and here they are."

Men cheered and beat their hands together.

"No, no," Steele yelled over their shouts. He waved his hand again. "If anyone earned it, it's Kepler. He would have been here two hours ago, but he wouldn't leave 'til we got the Indian out."

Only then did I realize the shouts had been for me. They helped me to the back of a wagon and hung a blanket over my shoulders.

Steele passed the stretcher to a miner. Mary Novatni caught hold of her father's shirttail. Novatni slipped his free arm around his little girl and hugged her close, but he wouldn't surrender his grip on Joe's stretcher. They slid Joe into the back of the wagon where I sat. The Indian's eyes rolled back at the jolt when they laid him in the wagon bed. I shook free of the blanket and touched the old man's face.

"I'm sorry," I whispered.

I pulled the leather pouch from the front of Joe's shirt, took a pinch of the cactus pollen, and sprinkled it in the air above his face. One of the miners jumped on the wagon seat. I nodded. The driver popped the end of the reins on the mule team and they lumbered off for the doctor in town.

"Thought you wouldn't have anything to do with that religious foolishness." Beard handed me a tin plate of cooked chicken.

"By what you believe, Sheriff, it might be foolish." I watched the wagon rattle over the bridge. "By what he believes, that dust in the air just might mean something."

I scooped my grimy fingers into the stew and stuffed my mouth full. Then dipped them in again.

"Careful there, Kepler," Beard said. "Might be bones in there."

"I'll eat them, too." I smiled up at my friend.

"See her there?" He raised his hand.

June stood by herself. The miners and their families bowed their heads as Father Dowd prayed.

"They tell me that gal waited right here with all the rest of 'em. Didn't even go back to May's when the word come that they found you and knew how to get you and the Indian out." The lawman rubbed his chin. "Eat your fill and we'll get you back to your place so you can rest up."

June tilted her head and then walked toward the bridge to town. The rags wrapped around her feet splashed in the mud.

After I had three plates of chicken stew in me, Beard took me away from the celebration at the mine site. He left me for a bath at the Chinaman's. I gave him the keys to my room at the hotel and he brought back clean clothes.

"Not many men would do what you did, Kepler," Beard told me on the ride back to the hotel. "You got a right to be proud of yourself."

Pride was the farthest thing from my mind. I shook my head. "You volunteered to go."

"Yeah, but you *did* go. Just when I think you're all about money, you show me you're not. In all that writin' you do, there never been a single word 'bout yourself. You're a strange man, Kepler. Killed Madison with your bare hands, then risked it all to save an Indian most people in this town wouldn't spit on." He pulled the wagon up in front of the hotel. "Get yourself some rest, you've earned that much."

And I kept water from Joe until he told me what I wanted to hear.

I should have fallen into the bed and slept for days. Instead I found a pen and paper. In the fading daylight, I lit the same lantern that Landry demanded be lit and composed a story about courage.

Not my own failing sort. Instead I told of men who each day faced the possibility of death deep in the mine to earn a living for themselves and their families. And when it was all on the line, how courage and love was all that mattered. I wrote about a man named Novatni, who returned to the black pit to rescue the Indian that saved his life; and about Mary Novatni, who thought her greatest joy would be to have new shoes that no one had ever worn before her, until she nearly lost her father.

It was after midnight when I finished. I wrapped myself in a coat and walked Brokeheart's back streets and alleys. At the newspaper office, I placed the story on Wilson's desk so it would be the first thing he saw in the morning.

On my way back to my room, I swore I heard a wolf howl.

Chapter Nineteen

"Kepler!"

The muffled sound of my name came through the closed door. A meaty hand pounded on the wood.

"Kepler, get up, man. You've slept the day away. It's nearly five o'clock. Open the door."

I recognized Wilson's voice.

"Just a minute." I stepped into my pants, shuffled to the door and pulled back the lock.

Wilson's face beamed. "I've never . . . We've never . . ."

"Never what?" I rubbed my eyes.

"Sold this many papers!" The fat man danced to my window and threw open the curtains. "I found what you wrote. I knew it was quite good." He straddled my desk chair and waved his hands. "I set the type myself and put the first two dozen papers on the morning train to Denver. I couldn't wait 'til evening so I put the papers on the street at noon. Sold out the first edition in no time." He jumped to his feet and paced. "Then the telegrams came in."

"Telegrams?"

"The papers in Denver want to run the story. The story you wrote." He grabbed his glasses before they fell from his face. "No doubt others cities will want it, too." His hands grabbed his flabby hips and he stared at me. "Well, get dressed. There's a celebration at the Catholic church. They're expectin' you. All the miners and their families.

They're using the word 'miracle.' Even found a goat to roast." He lumbered to the door. "It starts in an hour. Now hurry." And he was gone.

Shadowy silhouettes surrounded the blazing bonfire in front of the church. Off to one side, what was left of the goat turned on a spit over a bed of glowing coals. Yellow light spilled from the open door of the clapboard church. Around it people chattered and laughed.

From the bridge over Brokeheart Creek, I turned the collar of my coat up and looked back. I'd made my appearance, shook hands, accepted the pats on the back and pretended I enjoyed the undercooked, greasy slab of goat that a little gray woman brought me. I couldn't remember the last time I'd been in a church building, but I'd stood at the front, backlit by dozens of flickering candles, and nodded my head when Mr. Steele stumbled through a glowing account of what he called my "heroics."

Town leaders, who ordinarily wouldn't cross the bridge on a bet, stood solemnly during the prayers and speeches, then picked at the food the mine women had prepared. Wilson found a seat near the table of cakes and pies, perched a pad of paper on his bulging stomach and made notes.

I clamped my eyes shut for the first few words of Father Dowd's closing prayer, then stared at my boot tops until the final amen. I had started for the side door when little Mary Novatni dashed up to me.

"This dress was my mother's, she cut it down so I could wear it tonight." She caught the hem with fingers covered with cake crumbs, and half-curtsied. "But these are the shoes the man at the store said you left money for. I ain't never had real brand new shoes before." A missing front tooth showed in her smile. "Thank you for these shoes. Mama told Paulie to thank you for his, too. I don't think he will. And thank you for saving my Pa. I'm gonna thank God for you, Mr. Kepler, when I say my prayers tonight." She dashed off to join a group of girls her age. She pointed back at me then down at her new shoes.

Now I wanted to sleep. All that had happened caught up with me. My body ached and my mind wanted to surrender to the nothingness of slumber. But first, I needed a few minutes with Seer.

I turned my back on the church and clomped over the footbridge. Winter winds swept off the mountains and pushed me along. Just down the creek was where I had found Sophia's shoe before the rainstorm washed all traces of that terrible day away. Summer seemed like a lifetime ago. Landry had told me that the woman had been her first kill. Sophia's body lay buried on Graveyard Hill, not in the church cemetery where she belonged.

I blew all the air out of my lungs and watched the cloud fade away in the night air. And wished all I knew—but couldn't control—could fade away with it.

Seer whinnied before I pulled the door open. He stamped his feet on the fresh straw spread over his stall's floor and jerked at the halter rope when I touched his rump. I eased up beside him, tangled my fingers in his mane and rested my face on his neck.

"They think I'm a hero, boy. I don't know who I can tell. Who'd believe me if I did?"

The horse nuzzled my coat pocket. I chuckled and dug for the sugar I'd taken from the meeting at the church. His muzzle rested against my palm and we stood together in the shadowy stable building. I lit a lantern and hung it on a peg over his stall. With long, gentle strokes I pulled a curry-comb along his back and up his mane.

"He likes it when you do that." June stepped around the pile of straw and stood at the end of Seer's stall. She touched his back where the comb left its marks on his coat. "The man said I could come brush him down if I didn't cause no trouble. I asked him not to say nothin' to you. I had to do somethin' for him so he wouldn't tell. But just once."

"Didn't see you at the church party." I continued to pull the brush along Seer's back.

June patted his hair back into place after every stroke.

"May said wouldn't be no good for us to go. She said somethin' 'bout our kind bein' nervous in church." June draped both arms over Seer's flanks and rested her face on his back so she could watch me. "I read your words in the paper today. Knew about every one of 'em. Liked it a lot."

The lantern light made June's hair look almost white against Seer's sorrel coat. With the next pass of the comb, I caught the ends of her hair and tugged at them as I brushed the horse.

June twisted up her face and smiled. "I like bein' here with the horses. I forgets all the bad things at May's."

Seer tossed his head back. His eyes flared so that the white rims showed. The side door of the barn slammed open in the wind. Pewter-colored moonlight flooded in and a blast of cold midnight air followed. I caught June's arm and pulled her behind me.

"What would people think of their hero now? Playing in the stable straw with a little whore?" The door swung shut with a clunk. Landry pushed back the hood of her dark cape and wiped her mouth with the back of her hand.

The notion that she had been watching us churned the goat meat in my stomach. June's fingers clawed into the back of my coat.

"I told you I'd come back, Kepler." Landry glided towards us. She paused, then walked to the end of Seer's stall.

The horse fidgeted and pulled on his rope. He slammed against the side of the stall. I stroked his neck, trying to calm him. But his nostrils flared. I caught hold of his halter and pulled his head against my chest.

"I kept my word. I haven't said anything about what we talked about," I said to Landry.

She was different from that night in my room. The urgency was missing from her voice. The skin on her face was smooth as porcelain. Tortoiseshell combs held her dark hair back from her face. I could see no trace of the soft black hair above her lips.

"Nicolae grows restless," Landry said.

"What about you?"

"What do you mean?" Her eyes widened.

"I had some of the San Francisco newspapers sent here. I couldn't find any mention of cholera epidemics in the last twenty years. And there were other murders."

Purple flashed in her eyes. "Do you doubt me?"

June tightened her grip on my coat.

"What I think is," I said slowly, "is that you are just as guilty as him." I braced for what might come.

Landry touched a long finger to the tip of her tongue. She rolled her shoulders and pulled her lips back from her teeth. "We knew you were a smart man. Get one of the papers from Fairplay tomorrow. There's been another killing." She pulled the cape around her supple body. "Please keep your promise a bit longer. I think a storm is coming, Kepler. Oh, and tell the chippy, I like her cat."

She turned her back to us, crossed the stable, opened the door and slipped out. I could feel June tremble.

"Ain't she the woman from the train car? Is she gonna hurt Mister Buggs?" June cried softly.

"She's just trying to scare us." I turned and caught her shoulders and pulled her to me. "June, don't say anything about what you saw here. There's some things I need to do."

I hoped those words calmed her, for I had no idea what would come next. Maybe Nicolae and Landry would leave for Arizona Territory. Maybe if I kept my silence just a bit longer the evil Joe warned me of would be gone with them.

Wind cut through the gaps in the barn's boards. Straw skittered across the dirt floor. Seer snorted and the muscles along his back relaxed. June pulled away from me and wrapped her arms around my horse's neck. Through the cracks in the wall, I saw men with torches moving along the path to the church and into the creek bottom.

"Something happening at the church." I hurried toward the door. "Wait here."

Chapter Twenty

The lit torch bobbed in the man's hand. He stopped, held the flame above his head and scanned the alley.

I grabbed him by the collar and twisted his face up to mine. "What's going on?"

"Little girl turned up missin'."

"What?" I was nearly shouting.

"Her parents couldn't find her when things at the church started to break up."

"How long ago?"

"Maybe half hour."

I thought of Landry's fingers dabbing at her lips as she entered the stable.

"Help us find her, Kepler."

"Does the sheriff know?"

"Yes. Everyone is looking. I told 'em I'd see if she wandered over here."

I left him to search the alleys and streets on the town side of Brokeheart Creek and hurried toward the church.

Torchlight silhouetted Beard's tall figure. The lawman caught the handrail on the footbridge with both hands and peered into the darkness below him. His knees buckled and he clung to the railing to keep his feet.

"Stay back," he barked. "All of ya, just stay back."

Four miners with torches stopped short. A dozen more ran from the church. Father Dowd slipped by and onto the bridge. The priest's hand touched his forehead, then each shoulder.

"Keep 'em back, Father, 'til I'm sure." Beard turned and saw me. "Get a torch and come with me."

I snapped a torch away from a miner's hand and followed the sheriff around the end of the bridge and into the shadows along the creek bottom. Frozen grass crunched under our boots and brush grabbed at my face. Light from the torch flame cut the black into shapes and slashes of amber and gray. Although I couldn't make out anything in the darkness, Beard's eyes fixed on something ahead of us. He pushed through the tangles, his long arms slapping branches aside.

"Give me that torch." He reached back, jerked it from my hand and dropped onto his knees. "God in Heaven!"

I strained to see around the sheriff's broad back. He pulled an arm out of one sleeve of his coat, passed the light to his other hand and struggled out of the other sleeve. Gently he leaned forward and spread the coat over a figure on the ground.

"Her head's near tore off." Though it was a whisper, the words battered my senses.

I bent forward and rested a hand on the sheriff's shoulder.

In the yellow sputter of the torch, red splotches splattered the dirty snow and frozen leaves. Strands of dark hair peeked from the edge of Beard's coat. Frail little legs poked from the other end. New shoes that no one else ever wore clung to the tiny lifeless feet.

Beard never raised his head. He folded his hands together and bent his neck until his forehead touched his fingers. In words I couldn't make out, he pleaded with the God in Heaven.

Frost-coated leaves crackled along the edge of the gulley and voices seeped over the rim to where we knelt.

"I don't want her kin to see her this way." The lawman's hoarse whisper touched the night. "I don't want that undertaker to touch her, neither. Best get word to May that we need her."

Beard struggled to his feet and held the torch above his head. I couldn't take my eyes away from the dead girl's shoes. Just an hour before, little Mary had lifted the hem of her homemade dress to show me those very shoes.

"Sheriff?" It was the priest's voice.

"Father, keep everyone back," he answered. "We found her."

"Is she all right?"

"No." He brought the torch to his side and pinched the bridge of his nose with his free hand. "Get her folks and take 'em to your church. I'll be there directly and tell 'em what I know."

"They'll want to see her."

"Do as I say."

I thought I knew quiet. But as Beard's words faded away, silence took hold. Night animals ceased their movements, no bird dared flutter. Even the breeze refused to rustle a leaf. The thump of my heart paused.

Beard touched my shoulder and I moved my eyes away from the girl's ruined body. He lifted the torch ever so slightly. The flame's light brushed over a stark gray tree trunk a few steps away. A shiny rope-like strand swayed against the bark. Splotches of berry-red dabbed the tree. I tilted my head and studied the swinging tendril. Just higher than my head, June's cat, Mr. Buggs, hung impaled on a splintered branch. Its entrails spilled from a slash in its stomach.

Beard clamped his hand on my shirt front and pulled me to his face. The heat of the torch singed at my hair. Red veins webbed his eyes. "What do you know about this?"

I tried to make words come. My soul wanted to spew out all I knew. To tell how a wolf turned into a man. Landry's fingers on her lips. Joe's tales of shapeshifters. In the next instant, the sound of work boots grinding on the frozen gravel interrupted my stutter. A cascade of rocks tumbled from the edge of a gulley where the miners milled about and a woman's wail tore at the night.

"Keep back," the sheriff hollered at the gathering crowd. Then over his shoulder he snarled through clinched teeth, "Get that cat out of the tree and hide it where no one'll see. We'll talk in the mornin'."

Beard raised his hands and motioned to folks on the rim above us. "Stay back, nothin' to see here. Giuseppe, keep 'em away."

I pulled June's cat from the tree and wrapped its cool, limp body in my coat. Under a willow bush, I stuffed the bundle and covered it with leaves and old snow. The girl's mother's cries shook the night and the woman shouted pleas for her daughter to be alive.

I fixed my eyes on the torches and picked my way through the darkness and brush. I glanced back at the body covered with the sheriff's coat, grateful that the night hid it from me. I caught hold of a tree branch and lifted myself up out of the ravine.

A woman clawed at the ground and tried to crawl down the bank. Father Dowd pulled back on her shoulders. She beat at his hands and screamed louder. Another woman threw herself at the grief-stricken mother and wrapped her arms tightly around her. Together they sprawled in the dirt, clinging to each other. All was quiet except for their sobs. An emptiness swept over me and I shivered, but not at the cold.

I had to turn away and when I did, I saw Novatni and his wife at the edge of the shadows. I bolted from where I stood. Paulie clung to his mother's skirt. Novatni squeezed his wife's face into his shoulder. And little Mary, with her fingertips clamped on her father's belt, stared at the women on the ground. Wet marks, shining in the firelight, streaked her face. I hurled myself at Mary and caught her in my arms.

"I thought it was . . . the shoes . . ." I hugged her tight against my chest.

"I'm sorry. All the other girls were so jealous. I let them take turns wearing my new shoes," she whimpered. "Katrina wanted to. We were playing hide and seek. Nobody could find her."

"You're all right, that's all that matters."

"But Katrina."

"There's nothing anyone can do now."

I looked back at Katrina's mother. Her sounds were all used up but still she struggled to crawl down to her child's body.

"There's nothing we can do for her now," I whispered to Mary.

But my heart begged me to act.

May swathed Katrina's pale body in worn sheets she had brought from the Months. I fetched a pail of water from the creek. The saloon keeper's pudgy hands washed the blood from the girl's face as gently as an artist might touch a brush to canvas. In the lantern light, I watched May's own tears mingle with the dried blood. She wrapped the body in a new quilt and when I moved to help, she shook her head. May cradled the lifeless doll against her bosom and climbed the pathway to the church.

I stepped around her and held the door open. May touched her cheek to the precious bundle she carried. Miners' families filled the pews. All eyes turned to the big woman. May walked down the aisle to the altar and laid the girl there. The priest touched May's shoulder, but she brushed his hand away and hurried out.

As I shut the door behind us the wail of the women inside broke the silence. Over all their sobs, Katrina's mother's voice shook the windowpanes. Then the church's organ wheezed the first notes of a hymn.

"Kepler, I ain't seen June since the partyin' started here at the church," May said. "I told her it was best for us not to go. Figured she went anyway."

"I saw her at the stable after I left." I didn't say anything about Landry's visit.

"But she ain't never come back to my place, not after all the commotion started. You know how she likes to wander down by the creek at night lookin' for that cat of hers. That cat's 'bout all she has."

"Go back to the Months. I think I know where she is." I started for the footbridge and in three strides I was running.

Night skies faded and dawn traced the horizon. I clomped over the bridge and up the path to the stable. I vaulted the corral fence. Horses nickered and spooked away from me. My hand pulled the side door open. Lantern light sputtered and new sunbeams cut through the gaps in the slat boards. Seer tossed his head when he heard me. There in the straw at his feet, June huddled, fast asleep.

Relief swept over me. I knelt beside her and picked a shaft of straw from her face. Her eyes opened and she smiled at me. The horrors along the creek bottom seemed far away.

"Find Mr. Buggs, Kepler? That lady didn't hurt 'im, did she?"

I gathered her in my arms.

June tugged at my shirt and then snuggled her face into my chest. "What happened to your coat? It's cold out there."

"June, I need to tell you about Mr. Buggs." And I told her about Katrina and her cat and held her tight when she cried.

Chapter Twenty-One

By mid-morning, angry gray clouds draped the mountains. Wind-driven snow pellets peppered the town, bouncing off the clapboard buildings of Front Street and collecting in the wagon wheel ruts. Half the town knew that a miner's girl had died along Brokeheart Creek the night before. They shook their heads and frowned at the tragedy.

For the miners and their families, the loss was as cold and dark as the day. The happiness they'd shared over the rescue at the mine slipped away like the wind-hurried clouds off the icy peaks. Groups of twos and threes marched the path from their shanties to the church. Silently, they slipped in, said their prayers and lit candles for Katrina's soul.

I walked June back to the Months. May sent her upstairs and promised to watch her. At the general store, I bought a coat to replace the one I'd wrapped around the dead cat.

Two teamsters backed their wagon up to the loading dock of a warehouse off Front. They hitched a rope to the single tree and hoisted the carcass of a bull elk from the back of the wagon. The gash in the animal's neck looked too much like the torn throat of the girl. I turned my head, but a swirl of wind brought the musky smell of death to my nostrils.

A group of working men gathered around to admire the kill.

"Damnedest thing I ever saw," I heard one the hunt-ers say. "Snowed so much up high that we gave up huntin' and headed in. Just after sunup, we was no more than a mile from town and this old boy came plowin' up out of the willows." He tapped the blade of his skinning knife on the animal's side.

"Sam grabbed up his Winchester and drew down on 'im. The elk pulled up on the road not ten yards in front of us, and Sam knocked it down. I was slappin' ole Sam on the back when I looked up and saw this wolf. Like I said, damnedest thing." He looked at the men who had gathered around his wagon. "Purtiest damn wolf I'd ever seen. I think it chased the elk right to us and then it sat down on its haunches and just stared at us. Made my stomach turn. I swear its eyes was near purple color, and it had dried blood all streaked across its gray fur." He shook his head. "Sam emptied his rifle at 'im, but never cut a hair. It was like that wolf knew we'd never harm it. Then it just trotted off as pissy proud as could be."

"Just where did this happen?" I shouted to the man on the wagon.

"Up the road." He pointed with his knife. "Mile or so from the miner's church."

And a mile from the girl's body, I thought. The small hairs on the back of my neck stood on end. As if killing Katrina wasn't enough, now Landry chose to taunt me.

For much of my life, I had toyed with each day like a card game. Stay with the cards when they fell my way. Fold and run when my luck ran out.

My mother's words came back to me. "Complications are a part of life. Running from them only postpones the decisions until some other time or some other place." In Leadville, I had thrown away a train ticket and told myself that I would face the terror. But instead, I had traded a bit of myself for the life of a little girl. I couldn't keep what I knew inside me anymore.

I hurried from Front Street to the sheriff's office. Beard was on his knees beside his desk. His eyes were clamped tight and his folded hands rested near the open Bible on the desktop. After an instant, he looked up at me but never moved to stand.

"What you here to tell me, Kepler?"

"I know who . . . er, what killed the girl last night."

"Do ya, now?"

"The same thing killed the captain and Jeff. The woman, Sophia, two workers in the mountains, and at least three more in Leadville."

"First you said who. Then what. Now a thing? What are you talkin' about?" Beard eased up into his chair.

"It's not easy to explain. But every word is true." I reached out and let my hand rest on his Bible. "It started my first day in Brokeheart, but I was too greedy to see it."

For the best part of the next hour, I explained every detail of my relationship with Landry and Nicolae, every dollar they'd paid me and each torn body I had seen. Beard's eyes widened when I told him how the wolves turned into Nicolae and Landry before my eyes.

The muscles in Beard's jaws worked in and out but he never spoke until I finished.

The lawman tilted back and stared out his window. He rubbed his face, reached for the Bible and shut its cover. "I ain't supposin' to understand everything that you just told me." He turned and looked me in the eye. "Before you came in here, I was on my knees praying for two things.

Some sense of what was happening. And what to do about it."

I'd never thought I'd be the answer to a prayer. I wasn't sure I was now.

"We have to talk with Joe," I told him. "We need him to tell us everything he can about . . . them."

"He's still purty busted up from what happened in the mine. Doc's got him restin' up in a widow-woman's house so he can keep an eye on 'im." Beard put both hands on the desk and stood. He blew out a breath. "Do you think he'll talk?"

"Maybe to you. I'm not so sure about me."

Beard sent a sideways glance my way. "You have any idea where these *wolfmen* might be?"

"No. I've been thinking about that. Let's send word out and see if anyone's seen their train car."

The door flew open and cold wind rattled the pages of Beard's Bible. "Sheriff," a gaunt-faced man called out. "Better get over to the hotel, somethin' bad's happenin'"

The lawman grabbed his coat from the back of his chair and picked up his axe handle from against the wall. He turned to me. "Get yourself to the telegraph office and send out word on that train car. Then meet me."

"I can't, Kepler. Snow took down the line somewhere on the pass. We got to wait 'til they send a crew there to fix it." The attendant snapped his finger down on the telegraph key to prove what he said was true. "See there? Not even a hint of a signal. To top it off, the mornin' train is past due. We don't even know if it left Fairplay."

"When did you last get anything through?"

"First thing this morning. I gave 'em word on that miner girl bein' killed. The operator in Fairplay sent back that they found a woman all cut to hell on the train tracks."

My brain swam back to Landry's warning. "We knew you were a smart man." I remembered her lips and eyes as she spoke those words. "Get one of the papers from Fairplay tomorrow. There's been another killing."

The door of the potbelly stove clanged open. The telegraph operator tucked a shovelful of coal inside. He bent forward and blew until the fire glowed. "I don't like this one bit. The train's late. No telegraph. It's like we're cut off from everything." He pointed outside. "Look at that snow come down."

Flakes, big and wet, filled the air. Clumps of snow sledded down the windowpane, leaving wet streaks that turned to ice. And though it was two o'clock in the afternoon, it was as dark as night.

The wind pushed me through the hotel door. I stomped the wet snow off my boots, swept it off my shoulders and brushed the flakes from my face. Two boys, no older then nine or ten, perched on the front desk. The hotel clerk studied the boys and twisted his hands together. Beard leaned forward so his face was even with the boys.

The sheriff looked over his shoulder and motioned for me to come. A man and a woman, whom I guessed were the boys' parents, sat side by side on a divan near the desk. The woman dabbed at her eyes with a kerchief and the man fumbled with a pair of gloves.

Tears and phlegm mingled on the smaller boy's face.

He sucked in each breath in ragged gasps. The other boy rocked back and forth. All color had drained out of his face.

Beard shielded his mouth with a hand and whispered to me. "These boys snuck their daddy's shotgun out of the house 'fore daylight. They was goin' rabbit huntin' along the creek. Found a pile of bloody clothes out yonder. Woman's clothes."

Beard looked at me with hooded eyes. "The little one gathered up the clothes. Then they say a big gray wolf scared the bejeezus out of 'em." He looked back at the boys. The older one rocked faster. "It commenced to snowin' and they got all turned around. Can't say for sure just where they found those clothes. I want you to take a look and see what you think."

The man on the sofa mumbled something to his wife. She wiped at her eyes.

"Go ahead, boys," Beard said. "Get down there with your folks. You're in no trouble. Just had a passel of us worried. Everythin' settlin' down now."

In that fraction of a second, the boys sprung down and wrapped themselves in their parents' arms.

Beard turned back to me. "Whatever it was, those boys are more than spooked." He shook his head and whispered just enough for me to hear. "Think your she-wolf left another body out there? Findin' it in this blizzard isn't goin' to be easy."

I swallowed hard and whispered back, "We need to know." From somewhere, my brain conjured up images of another dead child.

The lawman nodded. "Get the boys home now," he said to the parents and reached out and tousled the littlest boy's head. "I want the two of you to take me huntin' with ya sometime soon."

He looked at the clerk. "Thanks for your help, but there's nothin' more to be done. At least 'til this snow stops."

Beard sprawled on the empty sofa as soon as the door shut behind the family. The tired lawman rubbed his eyes and bowed his head for a long moment.

"Sheriff, there's something else you need to know," I told him. "Telegraph wires are down. The morning train is late and there's no way of knowing if it even left Fairplay."

He blew out a breath and wiped a rough hand over his face. "Come on. Let's have a look at what those boys found."

Just inside the hotel's back door, an ugly lump of wet clothes spread out like old pancake batter on a cold stove. Beard knelt down, slipped a knife from his boot and picked up one of the soggy garments with the blade point. Red stains streaked the gray material. He flicked the blade and the dress slid to the floor. From the pile, he lifted a dark purple piece of fabric. He raised it above his head and I could see it was a hooded cloak.

I bit down on my lip. "We're not looking for another body. Those are the clothes Landry was wearing last night."

He looked up at me. The wet cloak dropped from the blade of his knife and slapped the floor. "What?"

"She must have changed into a wolf after she left."

"But the blood? It's gotta be that girl's."

"Landry left that so I would know. She's toying with me."

He turned his head away and looked at the floor.

"Oh, God," I whispered as my own words stung me.

"May He help us." And the sheriff began to pray.

The blizzard's wind made it hard to see more than two feet beyond my next step. Wet snow clung in clumps to my boots. Each footstep was heavier than the one before. Sheriff Beard plowed through drifting snow and I struggled to keep up. No other man or horse was on the street.

I followed him around the corner of a weather-washed house off Main. He pounded on the side door and a dour-faced woman answered. The wind pulled his words away before I could hear just what he said to her, but she swung the door open and I followed him inside.

"Miss Dawson's watchin' over the Indian." Beard took his coat off and wiped his boots on a scrap of rug laid by the door.

I followed his lead. "Ma'am, this here's Kepler. He writes for the paper. You might have read some of writin'."

Miss Dawson's hard face showed a bit of life. "I don't normally read the paper, but my friends mentioned your work and I have enjoyed some of your stories." She tipped her head. "Can I get you both something hot to drink?"

"I would appreciate that, ma'am." I forced my best smile.

She turned for the kitchen and the sheriff stopped her. "How's the Indian doin'?"

"He sleeps most of the day. But he's beginning to eat more. Why, last night I heard him chanting something." She tugged at a silver cross that hung from her neck. "Scared me terribly. If I didn't need the money so, I'd have him out of here."

"Yes, ma'am," the sheriff said. "We need to talk to him.

Just to see how he's doing. We'll go on back now, if it's all right."

"What about the tea?"

"We'll have it later, ma'am."

Even, measured breaths that blended with the wind from outside made the only sounds in the little room. Blankets bundled around Joe's face so only his forehead and a fringe of black hair showed. Beard swung a chair next to the cot and straddled it. He reached out and nudged at Joe's blanket-covered shoulder. The Indian lifted his head and opened his eyes.

"Joe? It's me, Sheriff Beard. I got Kepler with me. Need to ask you 'bout . . ." He glanced back at me, looking for the right word. "About what you know."

Joe struggled to sit up. He clenched his teeth and grabbed his leg. Blankets slid away and I could see that the doctor had tied a board to each side of Joe's leg with strips of rags.

"Leg startin' to heal up?" Beard asked.

Joe locked his eyes on mine. "Why he here?"

"Like I said, we need to ask you some questions. A little girl was killed last night. Kepler says you might know somethin' that will help us find who did it." The sheriff turned to me. "Why don't you see if Miss Dawson has that tea ready and bring Joe somethin' to drink."

"Water, Kepler," Joe said softly.

His words tore into my soul.

When I returned with a mug of tea for the sheriff and a tin cup of water for Joe, the Indian had propped himself up onto his elbows. The sheriff rolled a blanket and slipped it under Joe's back.

"I explained to Joe how you wouldn't leave the mine 'til

you was sure he was goin' to be all right. And I told him about what you said 'bout these wolfmen," the sheriff told me.

I held the cup so Joe could drink. "Shapeshifters," I said and looked at the Indian. "That's the word you used, Joe."

He lifted his lips from the cup and nodded.

"So they're real?" Sheriff Beard pushed the doubt from his voice.

"In your words," Joe began, "balance. Good and evil. When person seeks evil more than good, balance change. When evil is great, evil wins."

"So this Nicolae let evil take over?" I asked.

"Maybe him born to evil seekers. Sometimes families seek evil from generation to generation."

"Why wolves?"

"Maybe wolves choose them."

"Enough," Beard hissed. He stared out the window and the muscles in his jaws tightened. "I want to know how we can kill them."

"Fire," Joe said. "Burns evil to ash. Wind scatters 'til no more."

"You said something to me in the mine about silver."

"Pure metal from the earth. In old times, silver arrowheads kill wolfman."

Joe's head rolled back and he gritted his teeth. He fished the leather pouch from the front of his shirt. "Take this." His gnarled fingers reached out and dropped an object in my hand.

A yellowed tooth rested on my palm.

"Joe?"

"Wolf's fang. Much power." He slumped back on the bead.

My hand tightened on the tooth. "Get some rest, Joe."

Beard pulled the blankets over him. In a few minutes Joe was asleep. When I showed Beard the tooth, he looked away. Wind rippled through the gaps around the window and teased at his hair. The sheriff bent forward and rested his forehead on the window frame. "It's not what I believe," he whispered.

"Sheriff, it can't be about that now. You saw the girl. If we don't do something, there'll be more bodies. Next time they'll do more than scare those two boys."

He raised his head and looked out at the storm. "We'll do something, but where are they? With all this snow, how will we find them? They could be anywhere, waiting to attack."

I walked to the window. Wind caught the snow and blasted the house, rattling the window. I looked down at the wolf's tooth in my hand.

Chapter Twenty-Two

Certain that if the blizzard's cold didn't keep me awake, the horrors of the last days would, I huddled under my blankets and fought to stay warm. Icy air slipped through every gap of the hotel room's frost-coated windows. Shivers traveled my backbone. But sleep stalked in and found me like some dead thing.

Gray morning light jerked me from sleep's grip. I hung my coat around my shoulders and scraped away the icy film from the window glass. The blizzard had played itself out. New, white snow covered the rooftops and streets of Brokeheart. Wind picked up the frozen flakes and swirled them away like lost phantoms.

Across the creek, near the miner's church, three men with picks and shovels spilled black dirt onto the clean snow, preparing a grave for little Katrina. She would rest near the church.

The woman who died in July's heat so long ago lay in a frozen burial mound on Graveyard Hill. I wondered if her soul longed to be in the sacred ground of the churchyard.

Men bundled in coats and blankets waded the snowy streets. Drivers urged teams through the snow and smoke poured from every chimney. It was like the snow covered Brokeheart's awful secrets.

From my window on the second floor, I spied the slightest curl of dirty white against the bleak gray sky.

I rubbed the frost from the glass with my coat sleeve and squinted. The wisp became a plume of steam above a dark spot. The spot moved toward town, becoming larger until I was sure it was the train.

I pulled on my boots and hurried down the stairs.

By the time I made it through the drifts to the depot, others had gathered on the platform. Powdery rooster tails rose from the tracks as the locomotive plowed its way toward the station.

"Somethin' don't look right," a man beside me muttered.

The telegraph operator stepped out of the office, pushing his arms into his coat. He pulled open a brass spyglass and aimed it at the train. The telescope dropped from his eye, and he squinted and raised it to his face again. "They musta' dropped the freight cars, that's just the engine and coal car comin' in."

"How long will it take to get here?" I asked.

"I 'spect it'll be a half hour with all the snow they're pushing. Just can't figure what's goin' on."

"What about the telegraph?"

"Line's still down."

Filthy snow caked the sides of the coal car and icy lumps hung above the wheels. Rivulets of water ran from the boiler but turned to fragile icicles before they could drip from the steam engine. Three gaunt faces stared at us as the engine eased up to the platform.

"What in hell, Irish?" someone shouted.

The red-haired engineer jumped off the train. He pulled his cap off his head, bent over and grabbed his knees.

"Help them other two." He rubbed a dirty glove across his face. "They're frostbit bad."

Cinders and smoke settled from the sky. Others moved to help the two men from the engine. I slipped an arm over the engineer's shoulder and guided him inside the depot.

Sheriff Beard pushed in beside me and we lowered the red-headed trainman into a chair near the pot-bellied stove.

"What happened up there, Irish?" the lawman asked.

"Blizzard caught us at the top of the pass." The engineer took a tin cup of coffee from the telegraph operator. He held it in his hands for a long minute, letting the warmth seep into his fingers. "Snow was coming in sideways, the wind was blowing so hard. Drifts deeper than a man's head covering the tracks. I told the boys we'd sit tight in the mail car and wait her out."

He drained the cup in a single gulp and held it out for more. "Got any whiskey you can put in the next 'un?"

Beard took the mug and handed it back. The operator took a bottle from his desk drawer.

"Forget the coffee, just give me the bottle," Irish said.

Beard held his hand up to the telegraph worker. "Not until you tell me what happened."

The door flew open and the band of men started into the office. Beard snarled at the group, "Take those boys down to the Months and somebody get the doc. I'll send Irish down there after I finish with him." When the door shut, he said, "Tell your story, Irish."

"We sat tight 'til just before dark. The storm let up some. The conductor spotted that fancy train car on a siding up the line. You know the one." Irish looked at me. "That fella what's havin' the lodge built up there. His car."

Beard looked at me. Now we knew where Nicolae's car waited.

"Go on," I said.

"I could tell we weren't going nowhere, so the conductor gets this idea that he should go out and see if anyone's in that car. He remembered that dark-haired woman." Irish held his hands over the stove. "He started out. I swear the snow was hip deep. We watched him buck his way through the drifts." He looked at the sheriff. "Damn it, gimme some of that whiskey."

"Finish."

"He climbs up on the back and rattles the door. It pulls open in his hand and he screamed." He tugged at his beard. "I ain't never heard a man make that kind of noise. He comes runnin' back through the snow. Flounderin' somethin' awful. Babblin' 'bout dead people." He jerked his thumb towards the bottle. "Give me the whiskey."

The sheriff grabbed the bottle, splashed two fingers in the bottom of the cup and held it out to the engineer. Irish snapped the cup away and drained it.

"We pulled him up in the mail car and shut the door tight. He keeps on blabberin' about bodies and don't make no sense in what he's sayin'. I tell him to stay put. That me and the others are goin' over to take a look. I keep a Colt in my overalls. The mail clerk gets a rifle and my fireman found an axe." Irish held out the cup for more.

The sheriff shook his head.

"We head over to the car. Conductor cryin'and beggin' us not to. But he followed us." Irish looked up at the ceiling and continued. "We make our way over to that train car and I climb up with my pistol in my hand and swing the door open. It's dark in there. I strike a match. Damn it."

His vacant eyes locked on mine. "It looked like a slaughter house."

Irish bulled past the sheriff, grabbed the bottle and poured the whiskey in his mouth. He slammed it on the table and wiped his chin. "Pieces of men layin' everywhere. Arms and legs throwed on the floor. Skin peeled away from their ribs. Frozen blood splatterin' the walls. And three men's heads lined up on a table just a-starin' at us. Like somebody put 'em there just for us to find." He tipped up the bottle again. "I recognized one of those faces, Kepler. Rosie. Yeah, the man that was buildin' the house for that rich fella."

All Rosie wanted to do was a good job and to earn money for his family. Guilt swept over me for all the times I encouraged him to finish Nicolae's house.

Irish slumped in the chair. "I shut the door tight and we hightailed it back to the train. It was past sundown and dark under those clouds. The four of us was strung out in a line wadin' through the snow. Conductor was snivelin' and cryin'. He was behind me." He tipped the bottle to his lips. His tongue darted inside, lapping for the last drops. "A wolf came out the shadows and grabbed him by the throat. Just that quick, it drug him off. I pointed my pistol but didn't have time to shoot."

I looked up at Beard. He shook his head.

"After that we hunkered down in the mail car." Irish went on with the story, like he needed to cleanse himself. "We listened to that wolf howl all night. I climbed out at first light and fired up the boiler. I knew we couldn't push through the snow haulin' anything so I pulled the hitch pin and left the rest of the train there. The three of us got in the engine and we started down the hill. That devil wolf trotted down the mountain behind us, just out of rifle range. We hit the flat out there and another wolf joined him. When we got in sight of town, the two of them turned and loped off back toward the mountains."

The sheriff leaned against the wall and studied the snow-covered scene outside. "Irish, get on over to May's. Tell her to feed you and your boys. Tell her I'm payin'. For the whiskey, too."

The engineer stood up. "I ain't never saw animals act the way the wolf did. Like the whole time they enjoyed what they were doin'."

"Go on with him," Beard said to the telegraph operator. "Nothin' you can do here."

The two men hurried out into the cold winds.

"I'm going up that mountain," I said as the door shut.

Beard continued to stare out the window. "I'm goin' with you. We'll leave out just 'fore dawn. If we take that stock trail up the backside, that'll put us on the mountain at dark. 'Fore we go, we'll need some silver to melt down for bullets."

"I won some nuggets in a poker game last summer. I was saving them in case times got bad."

"Times is bad."

Chapter Twenty-Three

I promised Beard that I would meet him at the sheriff's office with the silver nuggets later that evening. He went off to check how the town fared after the blizzard. There were two people I needed to talk with before we left for Nicolae's mountain and I went to find each of them.

Father Dowd knelt at the altar where May had laid Katrina's body. Flames from stubby candles wavered in the breeze when I opened the door. He glanced back, saw me and struggled to his feet.

"Kepler, I'm glad you came," he said and walked up the aisle to where I waited. He wrapped a coarse wool blanket around his shoulders. Wisps of steam drifted from his nose in the chill air. "I wanted to ask you if you would say a few words at Katrina's service tomorrow."

I took my hat off and stared at the tops of my boots. A lump climbed from the pit of my stomach and filled in my throat.

I fumbled to speak.

"Are you all right?" Dowd reached out and touched my shoulder.

I shook my head and swallowed hard but it gave no relief.

"I can't." Those words fell from my mouth and shattered like ice when they hit the floor.

"The miners look to you for so much. What you've

written. What you did during the cave-in. It would mean much if you were to say just a few words to give them hope."

"No."

"Kepler, is something–"

"Listen, Father. I'm leaving Brokeheart and I might not be back."

"I don't understand . . ."

"On Monday morning, go to the bank. I've left a gift for the church. Use the money to help build a school for the miners' children." I looked at the question in his eyes. "One more thing. No one is to know where the money came from."

"Kepler, they should know. They will want to say thank you."

"Do as I say." I turned and left the church. Though I knew that the Katrina's open grave was just outside, I couldn't bring myself to look. And when I crossed the footbridge, I turned my face so I wouldn't look at the place beside the creek where we found her body.

The door to the Months was tied open in spite of the cold.

A fire roared in the fireplace and two tin stoves glowed almost red. An empty whiskey bottle laid on a table next to the face of the red-headed engineer. Raggedy breaths hissed from his mouth, but his eyes never opened.

May dished out stew from an iron pot and collected pennies for each ladleful. A line of a dozen men stood waiting their turn.

"Need some of this, Kepler?" she asked. "Real beef, not venison."

The smell made me remember that I hadn't eaten since the piece of goat meat at the church. "I'll have a plateful."

May filled a metal plate and handed the ladle to April.

"Make sure each of these pay you now." She frowned at the line of waiting men. "Some of these'd steal from their own mother." A smile curled her mouth. "If'n they knew who she was."

She waddled around the end of the bar and sat down at a table near the fireplace. I pulled up a chair and dug a fork into the food.

"The meat's stringy," I said, trying to chew.

"I said it was beef," May laughed. "I didn't say it was good beef. That cow mighta died in the blizzard for all I know."

"What's with the engineer?" I pointed the fork at Irish and then dug it in the stew.

"He came in a couple hours ago. Asked for a bottle. Finished it and asked for another. I made him eat some stew 'fore the third 'un. He just glared at the fire and drank. Keeled over a half hour ago. I've been keepin' an eye on him." She tapped her fingernails on the table beside my plate. "Somethin' happened on that mountain."

May didn't ask a question. She caught my wrist before I could get the fork into the stew. "Two other trainman did some talkin'. Irish shut 'em up and sent 'em back to the yard. Crazy talk. About wolves. You know anything about that?" She dug her nails into my skin.

I looked at Irish sprawled on the table. "May, I need you to do something for me."

"You ain't answering my question." She dug tighter and then let go.

"Just listen to me. I'm leaving town in the morning. And I might not be back."

"More crazy talk. From you now!"

"Listen!" I swallowed, reached out and put my hand on May's arm. "I'm going to leave some money at the bank. If I'm not back on Monday, the banker has instructions to give it to you."

May pulled her arm away.

"Please listen." Tears filled my eyes. "Use the money to take care of June. This is no place for her. Send her to Denver. Get her a place to live. Help her somehow."

May leaned close to my face. The smell of stale whiskey filled my nose. "What makes you so sure I wouldn't keep your money for myself?"

"Because I think you love June as much as I do."

"June's simple, Kepler." May touched a tear that ran down my cheek. "She needs someone to look after her."

"Please."

"Got a sister in Denver. Runs a boardin' house. Maybe I can get June a job with her. I'll do what I can." May touched my cheek again. "This have somethin' to do with that mountain and that dead little girl?"

I didn't answer, but I could feel May's eyes read my face.

"Are you gonna say it to June?" May asked.

"No, I don't want her to know anything about this."

"No, you fool. Are you gonna tell June you love her?"

Pinpoints of starlight painted the dark blue night. Wind set feathery clouds flying and sent a cold chill into the valley. Lantern light showed on the barred windows of the sheriff's office and piñon smoke flavored the air.

Beard's Bible was open and there was dust on the knees of his pants. The lawman wiped the barrel of his carbine with an oily rag.

"I brought the silver," I said, closing the door behind me.

From the leather sack, I dumped the nuggets on the pages of his Bible.

"Hopin' you'd have more. Melt this down and we'll have enough for maybe five bullets for the Winchesters." Beard shook his head. "Put the nuggets in the pot and let's see what we got."

"Sheriff, I want silver bullets for my pistol."

"Kepler, that gun of yours is made for shooting across a poker table, not for hunting wolves. I think we make up as many bullets as we can for the rifles."

"No, some for the pistol. With what's left, mold up bullets for your rifle. I don't think the gun they come out of is going to be that important. It's what they hit."

"You're gonna have to be real close with that pistol."

"I intend to be."

Beard scooped the nuggets from his Bible and dropped them in the pot on the stove. He gathered empty cartridges and a can of gunpowder from a cabinet and waited for the silver to melt. Then he poured the molten silver into the molds. After they cooled, he examined each shiny bullet. The ones that didn't meet his test, he melted again and repoured. An hour later he dripped the last of the silver into the mold. Two slugs near the size of my fingertip for his rifle and three pellets no bigger than a dried pea for my handgun stood in a straight line on his desk.

He measured the gunpowder, filled the brass shells and crimped the silver bullets in place. "David kilt Goliath with a stone. God's own hand guided that rock." He pushed my three silver-tipped cartridges across the desktop toward me. "Best get on over to the stable and get the horses ready."

The sheriff stood up and took his heavy coat from a deer antler on the wall. Before he buttoned it, he unpinned the badge from the front of his shirt and laid it on the desk. "Townfolks ain't payin me to chase wolfmen." The lantern light washed over his face and left dark shadows around his eyes. He gathered his gloves, hat, and rifle and then gently placed his Bible into the saddlebags he draped over his shoulder.

"Sheriff, you don't have to come. I can go myself. I'm responsible for–"

He slapped his gloves on his pant leg. "Kepler, I ran for sheriff 'cause folks hereabouts needed somebody they could trust. I preach at the church 'cause those same folks need to hear what the Book tells 'em. That's been my life. The law and the Book." He pulled open the door. The flames in the tin stove flared. "Whatever's up on that mountain needs takin' care of so's it don't hurt these good people ever ag'in. That's why I'm goin'. I'm just not sure why you are."

I sucked my bottom lip over my teeth and bit down until it hurt. "I can't find the words for this. I scoffed at those who preached to me about good and evil. But I've seen evil. Maybe by going up there I can pay for some of my own." I tucked the silver bullets into my coat pocket and followed him into the night.

The stable was dark when we got there. Beard threw a

saddle over a big barrel-chested gelding. "Take that long-legged dun for yourself."

"I'll ride Seer."

"Yours is too spindly-legged for this deep snow. He'll play out."

"I'm taking Seer."

"Made up your mind, haven't ya? You planned this out."

"Like a man writing his own will."

Dawn painted the mountaintops pink and orange. It colored each ripple in the clouds bright shades of red. To the east a sleepy white sun peeked over the horizon. Beard's big chestnut horse broke a trail through the snow. Seer fell in behind. Beard's mount plodded on with its head down. Seer held his face high as if he knew what waited on the mountain.

My moustache froze to the hood I'd made from a saddle blanket. The cold seared my eyes. Beard leaned forward in his saddle and pushed on. The steam from his breath mingled with his horse's. The branch tips of gray sagebrush pushed through the white mantle like stubble on an old man's chin. Neither of us spoke.

Too many thoughts crowded in. But one came back again and again.

I should have found June.

I should have told her.

The horses climbed from the valley floor to the soft snow of the timber. Aspen trees as white and stark as skeletons' bones hung over our path. Seer swung his head and stamped his hooves.

"Sheriff," I called out. "Look."

An elk, dragging its bloody haunches, limped away from us in the snow. It shook its head and fought to get away but only floundered more. Beard pulled his rifle from its scabbard and brought it to his cheek. The gunshot shattered the cold silence and then all was quiet again.

The sheriff reined his horse to where the elk fell. "A pack of wolves 'bout the only thing will take on a bull elk. After tearin' him up this bad I don't know why they didn't kill him."

We climbed higher up the mountain. Across the creek, three dark shapes littered a snow-covered meadow surrounded by aspens.

"More elk." Beard pointed. Hoofprints trampled the blood-stained snow. "This time they finished the job."

Seer's nostrils flared. I pulled up sharply on the reins, but he crow-hopped away from the dead animals. He lifted his head and whinnied.

"Sheriff, he's trying to show me something." Then I saw it. "There."

Dark yellow stained the snow at the base of a spruce tree and a musky odor filled the icy air.

Beard rode up next to us and looked down. "Markin' their territory. They want everybody and everything to know this here's their mountain."

The chestnut's hooves broke through the ice on the creek. Beard clucked to his horse and they waded across. We turned and climbed up the mountain, forging into the powdery snow in the dark pine timber.

In a clearing in the trees, Beard swung out of the saddle. "Best let these horses rest a spell." He took a sack of grain from his saddle bag and spread it on snow that he stamped down.

"Gather up some wood. We'll get a fire goin' and warm ourselves for a spell."

"Aren't you afraid they'll see smoke and know someone's coming?"

"They already know."

The sun sat straight overhead. Beams of light filtered through the shadowy trees, mocking us with light that promised warmth but gave none. Beard roasted venison chops over the fire we built. The meat charred black and sizzling grease dropped onto yellow flames. I bit off a mouthful, hoping food in my stomach would warm me. My belly revolted at the bloody taste of the undercooked meat. Too much like the dead elk we had passed on the trail.

We led the horses through downed trees, scattered like matchsticks cast aside by some great giant.

"Watch yourself," Beard called over his shoulder. "Slip on one of these icy blowdowns, and you'll have that horse on top of you."

Ice-cold air burned my lungs. I tried to speak. Words creaked out of my mouth and skipped away in the wind.

Beard's horse stumbled. Wood cracked like a rifle shot. The big animal shrieked in fear. The sheriff caught hold of the horse's bridle and fought to calm the brute. It swung its head and lifted the sheriff off his feet.

He pulled the horse to a stop and stroked its big face, all the time speaking softly to the wide-eyed animal.

Seer and I moved close to them.

"This horse got a noseful of that." He cocked his head at another yellow patch in the snow. He kicked clean snow over the urine stain, checked his saddle's cinch and swung up onto his horse's back. "We got a long ways more to go."

Seer never faltered, never missed a step. He kept his head up, scanning what was ahead, like he remembered this forgotten trail.

More dead elk. A coyote, nearly torn to shreds, lay beside the trail. Then deer. Necks twisted, throats ripped, yet not a bite taken for food. The blood-splattered snow was marked with wolf tracks.

"Like some kind of killing frenzy," I whispered, not believing what I saw. The tiny feet of ten thousand insects scurried down my spine.

At the top of the pass, where I had buried Rosie's two workers, Beard climbed down from his horse and tugged up the saddle cinch. "Best let 'em rest. It'll be dark soon."

I swung out of my saddle. Beard stomped a place in the snow and dumped out a bag of grain for the horses.

"I've been watchin' the tracks around the kills." Beard found the small of his back with both hands and stretched. "It appears that it's just a pair of wolves. A big set, I'm guessin' is the male and smaller tracks must be the woman–I mean, female."

"You still don't believe what I told you, do you?"

"Everything I have faith in tells me not to. But each dead animal we passed tells me I must." He tipped back his hat and wiped his forehead with the back of his glove. "Whatever it is in 'em, it's like they're crazy for blood." Beard rubbed his eyes. "How much farther?"

"Maybe three miles as the crow flies, but its switchback trail all the way. Twice that far for the horses."

"And in snow up to their bellies." He smacked his gloves on his legs and looked up. "Listen. Hear that?"

I strained. The horses crunched the grain and stamped their feet in the snow. Wind sifted through the treetops. Then a sound. Almost a sigh.

No, a faraway baby's cry.

Beard plunged away down the hill with me right behind. He lost his footing in the snow and pitched forward. I passed him, following the sounds to where young pine trees pushed up through the snow. I pushed the tree branches aside and stopped.

Blood and hair spread over the snow in front of me. A deer scrambled onto its front feet. I feared blood would flow from my ears from its screams. The little doe's front legs thrashed in the snow, dragging its useless back legs. Its hide had been peeled from its back, exposing shiny pink flesh. As it struggled to escape I could see its muscles and tendons flex.

I fumbled into my coat's pocket for my pistol. I leveled the gun at the deer's head, ready to end its torment.

Beard grabbed my arm. "No. Save your bullets." He pushed the gun down.

The sheriff caught the terrified deer by an ear and wrestled his arm around the animal's face. It shrieked and struggled to fight away from the big man. I heard the bones splinter as he snapped its neck. One front leg kicked and the deer slumped lifeless onto the snow.

"They're tired of killin'. Now those devil wolves want to see things suffer." Beard bent, put his hands on his knees and gasped for breath. "Kepler."

Between his boots, the barefoot print of a man was pressed into the bloody snow.

I fought the bile that rose in my throat. "They've

changed. Shifted shapes," I stuttered. "They were in human form when they did this."

Beard hung his head. I knew he wondered the same things I did.

Would silver bullets be enough?

Beard slapped the end of his reins on his horse's rump. But the animal balked at the deep snow.

"Let Seer lead," I called out. Seer kicked powdery flakes into the air as he lunged through the drifts. Without any pressure on the bit in his mouth, Seer found the shallow snow at the side of the trail and picked his way down the twisted path. Beard urged his mount on and followed.

Bright red droplets speckled the clean white snow. A rabbit with its leg ripped off squealed and tried to drag itself away. Beard swung from his saddle, caught the terrified animal and with a quick twist ended its suffering.

Footprints I knew to be Nicolae's and Landry's led down the mountain. I thought of the night Landry had visited my hotel room and pleaded for my help. My mind still held the image of the animal's fur covering the woman's body. I fought to believe that it must be that form that left these tortured creatures dying along the trail. I needed to think that nothing human could do such a thing.

Four more times, Beard left his horse to perform bitter mercy on some mutilated animal. Each time as he climbed back into the saddle, the determination on his face grew as dark as the coming night.

Are the events of our lives predestined? Or do they fall as randomly as cards around the poker table?

The sheriff believed that every moment had been ordered by his creator. There had been no question that he would come to this mountain to battle the evil that had slipped over the town and people he cared for.

Any sense of obligation held no such compulsion for me. My life ebbed and flowed with the weight of coins in my vest pocket. Words on a newspaper page: only a means to an end. Horses were to be enjoyed. Whiskey savored. Women dallied with.

Until Brokeheart.

Miners and their families. This man who rode behind me. And June. The things I'd come to love, and might never see again, had taught me much about myself.

In my greed, Nicolae had swayed me.

Beard had his duty to fulfill on the mountain. I sought atonement.

The wind stirred the pine trees and snow as fine as sugar showered the trail. Tortured rabbits, squirrels, and weasels seemed all around us. The fortunate had died swiftly. Not even the smell of brimstone from the lowest level of Hell could match the scent of the animals' blood in the air.

And still we rode on.

Chapter Twenty-Four

Beard looped the ends of his reins around an aspen tree. "We'll leave the horses here. Make sure they can't get loose."

I tied Seer to a tree and eased his cinch.

Beard squatted on his bootheels and picked up a broken branch. He traced a zig-zag line in the snow. "This here's the trail we just came down." He drew another arc in the snow and sprinkled pine needles over it. "This'd be that lake." He placed a pinecone on his map and looked at me. "And 'bout here is the buildin'. What else you remember?"

I took his stick and made three dots between the lake and Nicolae's lodge. "The worker's camp was here. I remember a creek that ran along here." I drew another line from the pinecone to the lake. "And this would be the road to the rail stop where they'd pick up the supplies."

Beard pulled off his gloves, blew into his fingers and rubbed his hands together. "We got about an hour more of daylight. I'm bettin' that as soon as the sun drops behind the mountain, it'll be black as sin in this valley."

"That's why he chose this place." Fear coiled around my throat like some serpent and slithered down my back.

Beard looked off toward the lodge. "Wind's in our face. They won't scent us. Let's pick our way through the forest and get a look at their house."

I patted Seer's flanks while the lawman pulled his rifle

from the scabbard on his saddle. We waded in knee-deep snow over a little ridge that protected the horses from sight of Nicolae's lodge. Beard motioned for me to stop. We knelt a dozen feet from where the forest opened up into the meadow.

I heard her voice before I saw Landry. Beard handed me his field glasses. I focused on the house a half-mile away. Landry stood behind a window the workers hadn't glassed in. Beams from the setting sun touched the chalice in her hand and a point of crimson blazed from the blood-red wine. I shrank down in the snow.

Nicolae appeared in the window frame. His deep laugh rolled over the valley and echoed back. He caught Landry by the arm and pulled her to him. Her mouth went eagerly to his. The wine from her glass spilled out the open window, sending red splotches onto the snow.

Beard took the binoculars and studied the house. Nicolae's and Landry's laughter cascaded through the valley.

"They don't seem all that worried 'bout us," he said. "Maybe they don't know we're here or they're too haughty to care."

"They're getting ready for the night's hunt." I took the glasses back and peered at the house. The window was empty. "I don't think they've satisfied their blood lust. They'll shift shapes and prowl and kill all night."

"If you're right," the sheriff whispered, "our best chance might be to sneak into that house and be waitin' for them in the mornin'. Just sit there and let 'em come to us."

A wolf's howl replaced the laughter. Then another voice joined the first. Golden spikes of sunlight shot into the sky as sun touched the mountain top. Inch by inch, the light in the valley went flat. Thick gray shadows filled in around each tree. Then a slate-colored moon slipped up over the horizon.

Nicolae lifted himself through the window. A purple robe dropped from his shoulders. He caught up a handful of snow, stained with Landry's wine, and rubbed it across his bare chest.

His head tilted back and he roared. The trees above my head seemed to shake in fear.

Nicolae rolled his shoulders. He dropped onto his hands and knees. Landry stepped onto the window frame. Nicolae reached up and tore the dress from her. Her laugh blended with his animal sounds. She stood, enjoying the cold wind on her naked flesh. Nicolae lurched toward her. His hands batted at the air.

Some strange funnel of wind lifted the snow around them. I took the binoculars back from Beard. The noises blended until a chorus of wolf howls filled the valley. From the cloud of snow, a gray wolf appeared, followed by a larger black beast. They loped across the shadowy meadow. The black wolf snapped at his mate's flanks. The pair turned and raced along the lake's edge away from us.

"God in Heaven help us," Beard said.

The night settled around us. We gnawed on the jerky meat Beard took from his saddle bags and draped blankets from our bedrolls over us. We sat back to back to share each other's warmth. Though my body convulsed with the cold, the only time I felt Beard shiver was at the death wail from some animal on the hill above the lake.

The sharp cries of coyotes turned to yips of pain. Then the wolves would howl over their trophies.

The clouds drifted overhead until gray moonlight filtered into the valley. Across the lake a herd of frightened deer fled the mountainside. The terrified animals dashed onto the frozen lake. Under the weight of so many, the ice gave way. Mournful bleats filled the air as they struggled to save themselves. All the while, the two wolves paced the shoreline.

"I can't stand it anymore," I hissed though my teeth and clamped my hands over my ears.

"Cut the horses loose."

"What?"

"We've gotta get to that house and wait for them to come to us. If we leave the horses tied up here, they'll have no chance. Let 'em go and hope the wolves are tired of killin' by the time they get back to this valley floor."

"How will we get back to Brokeheart?"

"God'll provide."

Beard tossed off the blankets and picked up his rifle. Moonlight glared off the blue steel. He pulled off a glove with his teeth and worked the lever of his Winchester slowly. He caught each of the cartridges. From his shirt pocket he took out the two silver bullets and thumbed them into the rifle's loading gate.

I pulled the saddle from Seer's back and stroked his neck. I whispered the only words that came to me: "Take care of yourself." I felt foolish and scared. But I took off his bridle and let him go.

Beard snatched a steaming horse turd from the snow. He smeared it over boots and around the legs of his pants. "Might help mask our scent. You do the same, Kepler. Then load that pistol of yours."

After rubbing the manure on my pant legs, I pumped

my fingers into fists to loosen my stiff joints and fumbled for the gun in my coat pocket. I broke open the action, clumsily lifted out the ammunition and then carefully dropped the three silver-tipped cartridges into the cylinder.

"Follow me," Beard whispered. "We'll stay in the trees. With this moonlight, I don't want to take any chance of 'em being able to see us if we get out in the open."

We climbed the hill to where we had watched Nicolae and Landry shift to their wolf shapes. Beard led the way and we skirted through the darks and grays of the shadowy aspens.

"Slow down," he hissed. "Crust on the snow is making too much noise."

As carefully as I could, I moved along. One step in three, the crust held. With the other two I dropped past my knees. Frigid night air wrapped around me. Shroud-like clouds clung to the moon, then whisked away in the freezing wind. Like the light of a burning pyre, a moonbeam sparkled off a tree branch.

Beard held up his hand and then pointed. A snow-capped, rusty lantern hung from a spike driven into a tree trunk. "See it?"

"This is about where the workers picketed the horses and mules," I whispered.

"Check that lantern. If there's any coal oil left in it, we'll take it with us. Might need light to track a wounded one down. No way we can let one get away."

I struggled through the snow, reached up and took down the oil lamp. The wire bail burned cold through my glove. I held the lantern to my ear and sloshed the oil. Nearly half full.

My boot slipped off a snow-slick rock. I grabbed the

tree to keep my balance and kicked the snow away to stop myself from slipping again. Two dark spots stared up at me. I stared down and the pits became hollow eye sockets.

"Beard!" I breathed out.

He snapped the rifle from off his shoulder and waded to where I stood. I pointed down.

"One of the workers," I said through my teeth.

"Is there no end to their killin'?"

"Rosie had maybe eight men up here," I told Beard. "Irish said there were three bodies in the train car. This makes four."

"Five." He pointed with his rifle. A shriveled arm poked from the snow a few paces away. "And a mule, there. Picket rope still around its neck." Its lips curled back over yellowed teeth in a grim death mask. "I'm guessing those humps in the snow are the rest of the work animals." Gray light caught the contours of a dozen bumps in the snow.

I watched where I stepped, careful not to disturb another body, and followed the sheriff away from this place of death.

The higher on the hill we climbed, the softer the snow became. Take a step. Sink to my thigh. Wrestle my leg free. Take the next step. Beard's great size forced him to labor more than I did. While I groaned with each exertion, I never heard a sound from him.

Near the top of the hill, Beard held up his hand and we paused. The moon shone down from straight overhead. Nicolae's house sat less than a hundred yards from us. The front door hung open on hinges that squeaked with each hint of breeze in the still valley air. A muddy path led through the snow to the front door. Around the path, wolf tracks mingled with urine stains and the barefoot prints of Nicolae and Landry. Dark blotches, almost black on the white snow, seemed to be everywhere. In this world of shadows and grays, I could only believe those stains were blood.

On one side of the house, moonlight sparkled off the neatly stacked window panes that had never been placed in their frames.

A handsaw sat on a window sill. An axe leaned on the railing. I wondered if the man I'd found near the lantern had used those tools.

Shadows and shapes changed as a cloud fled across the moon. On the mountain above the lake, Nicolae's deep voice howled. Then Landry answered. Cold tickled the hairs on my neck.

"They're comin' down the mountain," Beard said, pushing at the brim of his hat with his rifle's muzzle. "Let's get to that house. We'll go in one of them back windows, so we don't leave our smell 'round that door."

The smell of death and animal filth oozed from the blackness inside Nicolae's half-finished house. The stench was so thick that I felt its oily film on my skin. Moonlight flooded through a front window in the great room. I stepped over piles of animals' bones—most with hide and fur still attached. A steamer trunk spilled women's clothes across the staircase.

Half-empty bottles of their bloody wine littered the floor. My throat clamped shut remembering the night Nicolae had offered me a glass.

"They could come in any of these windows or doors."

Beard squinted in the darkness. "Let's get up those stairs to the landing and hide. Don't touch anythin'."

Beard followed me up the flight of steps. He paused to pick up a torn deer hide and dragged it over the stairs where we had stepped. We crouched down behind a pile of lumber at the top of the steps. Beard peered over the stack and aimed his rifle at the front door, then each of the windows.

"Can you see well enough to shoot?"

He shook his head. "It's too dark for a clean shot. Maybe we'll have some light by the time they get here."

I bit down on my lip. The room's foul smell left a taste on my tongue. "Do you think they'll come as wolves or people?"

This wasn't the first time I had faced the chance of my own death. I had been faster with my pistol than the gambler across the poker table. When the stagecoach tumbled into a river, I was the only passenger to find the bank. In the bare-handed fight with Madison, a fury welled up inside and saved me.

A half-second or a half-inch one way or the other and the fates could have turned differently. But in each of these events things of this natural world held sway. My own avarice and the gambler died. A broken bridge timber and six lives swept away. Madison's rage, his own demise.

I feared that these creatures from the other world would not be limited by things of this earth.

Perhaps the God that Beard prayed to had spared me for these coming hours.

Beard touched my arm and leaned close. Mist seeped from his lips and filtered through his mustache as he whispered, "I'll shoot first. Don't fire that pistol 'til we need it. I'll wait until they're both inside. I need a clean shot at one and then the next. If I miss, then use that pistol. But not 'til then, hear me?"

Chapter Twenty-Five

My chin touched my chest and I snapped awake. Moonlight reflecting off the snow filled the windows. Sheriff Beard laid his pocket watch on the lumber in front of us. Twenty after two. We'd been in the house for nearly four hours.

Beard pushed the lantern against the woodpile in front of us. "Do you have matches?" he mouthed.

I dug under my coat into my vest pocket. My fingers touched matches and the smooth surface of the wolf's tooth Joe had given me. I nodded to the sheriff.

He touched the lantern. "Keep those matches dry."

I pinched Joe's wolf tooth tight.

Shadows stretched in the gloominess. At every shift of light I imagined a wolf sneaking closer. The smallest whiff of kerosene mixed with the thick odor of death that filled the room. I forced myself to exhale. Air seeped from my mouth in a ragged series of puffs. Wind slipped through the glassless windows. Its cold tongue licked me. I wondered if my numb fingers could pull the trigger when the time came.

The wolf's howl changed me. My heartbeat pushed warm blood into every fiber of my being. All my senses stood on edge.

Then horses. Two animals screamed. I recognized Seer's sounds. I strained to hear more. Maybe hoofbeats in the deep snow? I couldn't be sure. I had struggled in the snowdrifts. Seer would bog down and be easy prey for the wolves. Then all went quiet.

Beard's big hand found my arm. "Steady yourself."

I bit down on my lip. His plan was wrong. If they came through the door we would be trapped. There was no way to see them in the dark. What if the silver bullets were religious foolishness? Tales told around a campfire? We needed to meet the wolf-creatures in the open. Just at dawn. They would be tired from the nightlong hunt. We should be hiding outside in the trees and attack as they came back to the house. Not cornered in their lair.

Moonbeams shined on Beard's watch, but the hands wouldn't move. Seconds seemed like hours. Down below us, the cold metal hinges on the open door moved a bit. The metal whined like a dying cat. The door moved again and a mournful, ragged screech hurt my ears. A single wolf howled to answer the sound.

The muscles in my legs cramped. I wanted to move, take Beard and hurry from this place, face the wolves in the open where we'd have a chance.

The sheriff's hand squeezed my arm. "Wait, they'll come to us."

Clouds swept across the moon, stealing the gray light and turning everything black. Hinges groaned and a hint of moonlight touched the corners of the front window. All the horrid smells–decaying meat, the horse dung on my pants, animal filth–caught in my throat and I wanted to gag. Blood pounded in my temples.

Beard tapped my wrist three times.

I squinted at him. His silhouetted face fixed on the doorway below. He lifted his rifle to his shoulder.

Outside the door, one snow crystal at a time compacted

under the weight of a demon's paws. The fiend's nose sniffed the air, searching for what had betrayed its home. From deep in its paunch a growl floated on the still air.

The lawman steadied his elbow on the pile of lumber and tucked his cheek against his rifle's stock. I brought my pistol up and pointed at the door. In the dark, I could not be sure.

The growl deepened. The beast's nose sniffed in the air, straining at the strange scent. My scent. In spite of the cold, a drop of sweat ran down my forehead.

The monster's claws scratched the doorframe. The air in the house moved. It swirled around us and down the stairs. Dust and animal hair grazed my face. The growl turned to a moan, like a man would moan in pain.

It's changing. Shifting shapes. It won't be a wolf. It's coming as a man.

Suddenly, through the front window the sleek, gray wolf bounded onto the floor below us. Its sharp howl stabbed my ears. It reared onto its hind legs, silvery light reflecting on its purple eyes. A noise like a woman's scream filled the room. The refuse at its feet churned and lifted in a swirl of dust, snow, and animal bones. The unworldly creature dropped to its knees and Landry's face peered up at me.

The front door swung open, slamming into the wall. A hulking shaped stumbled out of the shadow. Nicolae stretched his neck from his rounded shoulders. His hair-covered face twisted up at me. I saw his nostrils flare.

Orange flames shot from the muzzle of Beard's rifle. The gunshot smashed the night into tiny pieces. Landry cried out. Her body twisted and her teeth snapped at the bloody wound blossoming on her side.

Beard lunged to his feet. "I can't see the other one," he yelled. "Use your gun. Put a bullet in that woman."

"I can't see it," I yelled.

I heard Beard's boots on the stairs. "Get the lantern. Follow me." He jacked the lever of his rifle and the spent cartridge hit the floor. "She's hit hard. We'll finish her later."

Shadowy images took shape again. I grabbed the oil lamp and kicked over the lumber pile. I stumbled and caught myself on the railing. The lantern clanged on the wood, but I kept my grip.

At the bottom of the stairs I pointed my pistol into the shadows and listened for any sound from Landry. Darkness wrapped around me, and I backed my way to the door. Outside, Beard waded in the snow searching for Nicolae's tracks.

"Light that lantern." he hollered, moving farther from the house.

I pushed up the glass globe and touched a lit match to the wick. A spot of flame took hold. Slowly a golden brightness spread in front of me.

"Come on, we got to find him before he can get away," Beard called.

I turned back to the open door of the house and lifted the light, trying to see inside.

"No time for her," he called again. "He could change back into a wolf and we'll never find him."

As if the master of all Hell had heard those words, the wind swirled in the trees on the hill. Out of the current of air, Nicolae's voice swept over the forest in a scream that turned into the animal's call.

Beard's long legs lunged toward the sound, churning

the snow behind him. I ran after him. The lantern swung wildly in my hand. The flame sputtered. Its circle of light faded then flared.

I caught the sheriff as he paused at the edge of the trees. The trunks of the pale aspen slashed angles in the darkness. My hands trembled. I fought to catch my breath and clung to the pistol in one hand and the lantern in the other.

"If he's a wolf, he can see better in this black then we can," Beard whispered. "If he's still that half-man monster I saw in the house, no tellin' what he can see or do. No doubt he knows where we are from that light."

I lifted the glass to blow it out.

"No," Beard said, taking the lantern from my hand. "We're goin' to follow these tracks and hope we can catch 'em. Keep your ears up that he don't slip around behind us."

I turned my face and peered into the trees.

Beard tapped his rifle on my shoulder. "I'm bettin' we'll hear him 'fore we ever see 'im. We'll take it slow as we can."

In the flickering light of the oil lamp, Beard looked at the barefoot prints of a man in the snow. He motioned with his rifle. "Come on."

Just minutes ago, fearing being trapped in the house, I had wanted to face the wolves in the open. Behind us, in that house, one lay dead or dying. Ahead of us in these dark woods, her mate could be stalking us. Now the only sounds were Beard's feet in the snow and the blood coursing through my veins.

Beard followed Nicolae's tracks for a few yards, then stopped and looked down. Pine trees replaced the aspens. Their dark needles stole away all the moonlight until only a dome of amber from the lantern gave any chance to see. Beard nodded and we moved on.

The trees swayed overhead and I flinched as their shifting shadows tricked my eyes. A branch snapped in the distance. Beard stopped and listened, then motioned for me.

"Kepler, look at this." Beard pointed. I lifted the lamp so I could see. Instead of the clear footprints in the snow, only the toes of the man's foot left their impressions. I held the light higher and Beard pointed his carbine at more marks in the snow. Nicolae's handprints pressed deep into the snow. Extended from the three middle fingers, scratches made by razor-sharp claws cut the ground.

"He's walking on all fours."

Where the coal-oil lamp threw its light into the forest, a kaleidoscope, not of colors, but silhouettes and gloom came alive. Gray snow, dark tree trunks, and green-black pine boughs hung all around us. Up above, moonlight grazed treetops. In any shadow the wolf-man could be coiling to pounce.

The tracks faded in a patch of snow-covered juniper. We circled the brush and cut the tracks further up the mountain. Marks where long fur brushed the snow plainly showed around the handprints.

"He's circling back toward the house," I told Beard.

"These tracks are out in the open." He gestured at the clearing in the forest. "Like he wants us to find 'im."

I scanned the opening in the trees.

Beard grabbed my arm. "Tracks lead back into the timber. I'll follow. You hang back. Keep me in sight, but not too close. And have that pistol ready."

I tightened my grip on the pistol and curled my thumb around the hammer. Beard walked off until he was another shadow among the grayness. The light from the lantern in my hand might keep the animal away from me. Like the slaughtered elk we'd found on the mountain, Beard offered himself as bait.

Branches tore at my face and coat as I followed him. Beard became a mist in the trees. A glimpse here. The snapped stick there. A little farther on his whole body came to my sight.

He'd watch the tracks in the snow, then study their path in front of him and move a few more steps.

I paused and leaned against the trunk of a pine tree. I breathed through my nose, trying to calm myself. A sour odor filled my nostrils. I jerked the lantern up and stared at the snow around my feet. At the base of the next tree, not five feet away, fresh yellow urine stained the snow.

Somewhere in the forest, Nicolae had moved between Beard and me.

Through a gap in the trees, I saw Beard turn. Before I could call out, Beard brought his rifle toward his shoulder.

Shadows came to life. The rifle fired. Flames from the muzzle shot upward. The precious silver bullet smashed into a tree. Fine snow showered from the tree branches.

In a blur of motion, the rifle flew from Beard's hands. He flung his arms up to guard his face and throat. I ran through the deep snow. The lamp in my hand swung with each step. In a flash of its light, the fallen snow sparkled on the black fur of the wolf-man. The animal caught Beard's arm in its jaws. I stopped and threw up the pistol. My arm shook. It was too far to risk a shot. I might hit Beard.

I pushed branches away from face and stumbled over a snow-covered log, hurling myself toward Beard and the monster. Beard screamed in pain. One of his hands clamped on the beast's throat. The other was still locked in its teeth.

My hand caught the trunk of a tree and I pushed myself

closer. Growls that chilled my blood filled the night. I lunged forward and jammed the muzzle of my pistol against the demon's side and pulled the trigger.

Nicolae's wail of pain ripped from the beast's mouth. Fangs flashed at me. Nicolae threw Beard aside. I fired again. In a frenzy of soul-piercing yelps, the wolf-man fled into the shadows.

My chest heaved in and out.

"Follow him!" Beard called from the flattened snow. "I'm all right. Finish him. Go."

I lurched through the bloody snow. Deep drag marks and footprints led down the hill back towards the house.

"Kepler, you have one bullet left," Beard called. "Make it count."

I could hear Nicolae gasping for air. Frozen sticks cracked under his weight. I stumbled and fell to my knees. The lantern nearly slipped from my hand. The marks in the snow led down the hill back toward the house, like a fox fleeing for its den.

I heard Beard stumble through the brush behind me, but I couldn't wait. The tracks led to the meadow above the house. I could see the half-man, half-wolf dragging itself across the open snow. Still too far away for my last shot.

Somewhere in the trees, near the lake, Seer whinnied. My horse loped into the snow-covered field. In the gray-white moonlight, Seer tossed his head and reared. As if I had called for his help, Seer charged the wolf-man.

"No," I screamed. "Seer, stop."

But my horse bore down on its mark. Nicolae struggled harder through the snow. I ran for all I was worth.

In full stride, Seer caught the wolf-man and bowled the ghoul over. The horse reared and his hooves, flailing, smashed down on Nicolae. Dark blood spurted from the beast's battered head. It roared in pain and dragged its body towards the open door of the house.

My last strides brought me to Seer. I pushed him away and pointed the gun at the door. Through the black opening I could see nothing. I stumbled forward and heaved the lantern in through the door. Glass shattered and kerosene spilled onto the wood floors. Flames followed the spilled liquid. The fire climbed the stairs and licked at the roof.

The walls caught and the inferno belched toward the sky. Flames filled each window and their heat seared my face. Through the doorway, in the midst of the hellfire, the wolf-man drew himself onto his hind legs. In a swirl of flames, the hair burned from its face and I stared into Nicolae's purple eyes.

I leveled the revolver at the tortured creature and cocked back the hammer. Beard stumbled up behind me.

He pushed the gun down. "Let him burn."

Beams and joists crackled. Flames ripped through the roof.

The tormented chorus of all the condemned of Hades could not compare with the death howl of the wolf. The building crumbled and the sounds of the wolf became the scream of a man.

The heavens had heard Beard's prayers. When dawn came, the earth and sky joined together to repent of all the evil that had happened before them. Golden sunlight shined from the vivid blue. The snow on the mountains glowed white and pure. Only the burnt black rubble of the house bore any evidence of the sins of this valley.

I looked at the yellowed wolf's tooth in the palm of my hand. Perhaps it had saved us. Or was it Beard's prayers?

Beard's heavy coat had protected his arm and the cuts left by the wolf's teeth were not deep. I bandaged the wound with strips of cloth from my own shirt. When I went to retrieve our saddles, I found Beard's chestnut horse hiding in the willows by the lake.

We feasted on hardtack and jerky and drank water from the creek. It was ice cold and clear as crystal, but no wine served in the finest hotel could taste as sweet.

Waves of heat still stirred the charred ruins as I saddled the horses. Beard rested against a scorched tree.

"Kepler, you have a story to write. What happened here should be told."

Wind swept off the mountains, stirring the ashes. I left the horses and walked through the cinders. Heat rose through my boot soles. With each step, white soot as fine as powder lifted and blew away.

"I want some proof. A piece of bone. Something, so I'll know they're gone and all this will never happen again."

Beard struggled to his feet. "Hell swallowed 'em up and we smelled its brimstone."

I helped the good sheriff onto his saddle and mounted Seer.

"Tell the story. It's like a duty, Kepler. Some will believe and some won't. Tell what happened so everyone has a chance to know."

I tapped my spurs to Seer's sides. Beard's chestnut fell in behind us. My mind tried to find the words to form the first line of the story. Where to start? In Nicolae's train car the night he offered more money than I believed I could ever earn? Or in Leadville where two wolves dashed from the forest and saved my life? In the mine when I tortured an injured man? When I watched a mother wail for her mutilated daughter?

Only the mountains and Beard's God could hear me. "Oh, I'll write the story. But not yet."

Epilogue

Paul Novatni looked down at black slate in his hands, then stared up at the children in the classroom. Two boys in the front row tried their best not to laugh but sounds creaked out of both mouths.

"Go on, Paul," I told him.

"My father," Paul whispered.

"Louder so everyone can hear."

The two in the front row struggled to contain themselves.

"Boys." I slapped my hand on the desk. "Go ahead, Paul."

Paul looked straight ahead and raised his voice. "My father is the bravest man I know. He was in a cave-in at the mine and saved the Indian's life. He still goes to work in the mine so we have food to eat."

Down the hill, the miner's end-of-day whistle blew.

Paul looked around. "And that's all," he said.

"That is all." I stood up from behind the desk. "Thank you, Paul."

The children gathered up their belongings. Paul's sister, Mary, called out from her seat in the back of the new schoolhouse. "Aren't you going to tell us one of your stories, Mr. Kepler?"

The school teacher said, "We don't have time today, Mary. But Mr. Kepler will be back with us next Friday, as he always is, to help with your vocabulary and writing. Tell Mr. Kepler thank you and I'll see you all on Monday morning."

"Thank you, Mr. Kepler," came back in unison, and students scrambled for the door.

I gathered my papers from the desk, put on my hat and followed the boys and girls outside.

The footprints of two dozen children from the miner's shanties trampled the mud path. The first signs of spring painted a green tinge on the cottonwoods along Brokeheart Creek. The snowline moved farther up the mountains each day.

A man on the footbridge raised his hand and called my name.

One arm of his coat was knotted just below the elbow and the empty sleeve swung as he walked toward me.

"Kepler, my name's Collier. We met in Leadville last fall. I was a clerk at the hotel." He wouldn't let his eyes quite meet mine.

"I remember you. What brings you to Brokeheart?"

"Editor Thomas asked me to bring you this." He held out an envelope.

"How is Thomas these days?" I took the packet from his hand.

"He bought his very own newspaper down in Arizona Territory. Town called Vengeance. He hired me to help move his family down there and I'm on my way back to Leadville. Train'll be leavin' soon so I got to hurry." Collier fidgeted and looked at the ground. "He paid ten dollars extra to bring that to you. Must be important." The train whistle sounded. "Best be getting back to the station." He backed away.

"Did Thomas say anything else?"

"He said give that to you and you'd understand. Don't rightly know what he meant by that." He tugged on the empty sleeve of his jacket with his good hand. "I need to go." With that he whirled around and scurried across the bridge.

In Leadville, Thomas had told me if I ever grew tired of Brokeheart he'd have a job for me there. That's what this was about, Thomas needed a reporter in Arizona.

Collier shot a look back from Front Street and then ran. He disappeared behind the buildings.

Without thought, my free hand dug into my vest pocket. My fingers found the yellowed wolf's tooth and the unfired silver bullet that I always carried since that night on Nicolae's mountain. I pulled my hand away and tapped the pocket.

I looked down at the envelope. There were no markings. Just a plain paper wrapper. I took a deep breath and tore it open.

Three neatly trimmed sheets of newsprint were folded inside. I undid them and looked at the top page. Being a newspaperman, my eyes settled to the top corner of the sheet to see which newspaper had printed the story.

The Dispatch: Vengeance, Arizona.

A detachment of the Fifth Cavalry came upon the homestead of the Henry Travis Family. All buildings had been burned by hostile Apache. All four family members were reported murdered. By the times the troops arrived, the bodies had been ravaged by marauding wolves.

I flipped to the next page.

Bisbee Chronicle

The supply train to the Henderson Mine was set upon by Apaches. Miners who came upon the gruesome scene days later report that the murdered men's bodies had been fed upon by wolves.

My tongue ran across my dry lips. I swallowed hard. The next page made the blood in my veins run as cold as that night on the mountain.

There was no writing. Only a grayed ink picture of a street in some desert mining town. The sign on a building in the background proclaimed "Vengeance Dry Goods." Dark hair hung from a woman's bonnet. By her figure I guessed her to be no more than thirty, yet she used a cane to help her walk. From the smudged face on yellowed paper, my eyes conjured up the slightest purple gleam in her eyes.

Publisher Wilson hooked his foot over the bottom rail of the corral. When he leaned forward his great stomach pressed against the fence. "So you really are going to leave. I told my wife I didn't think you'd do it."

I gave Seer a swat on the rump and the sorrel horse trotted up the ramp and into the train car.

"Thought old Beard would come into town to see you off." Wilson met me as I closed the gate.

"I went out to see him day before yesterday. Joe's out there helping him with the horses. He seems happy. He has a contract to supply mounts to the army."

"Never could understand why that man would just leave his badge on the desk and walk away. Sheriff one day and next thing he's building a ranch house out there in the valley. I never see him in town. Just sends that Indian in for supplies."

"His Bible was lying on the supper table. And there was dust on the knees of his pants from kneeling to pray like always. We talked a long time."

Wilson stuck out his hand. "Well, I best leave you now." He nodded down Front Street. "Other folks comin' to say their goodbyes." He pumped my arm. "You know you have a job with my paper if you ever need it." Wilson tipped his hat and walked off.

May had her arm over June's shoulders. "Knew you'd never stay in this town for long." The big woman squeezed June tight to her side. "Your kind never do."

June laid her head on May's shoulder. Dried tears streaked her freckled cheeks.

May kissed the top of her head. "Best be gettin' on that train, Kepler. It won't wait. Even for the likes of you, it won't." She put out her hand to take mine. It trembled. June wrapped her arms around May.

"Now, child." May caught June's face in her hands. "We done said our goodbyes. You just be goin'." Her voice cracked. "Kepler's a fine man. He'll look after you." She put June's tiny hand in mine.

The big woman plucked a cigar from the folds of her dress, flicked a match with her thumbnail and lit the cigar. Smoke lowed from her nostrils. "You take good care of our little girl, Kepler." And she walked away.

I helped June onto the steps of the train car. She grasped the window frame and watched May. Fresh tears seeped from her eyes. I led her to a seat in the empty car and put my arm around her shoulders.

"It's not too late. You can stay here with May."

She shook her head and laid it against me. The whistle sounded and the train lurched away from Brokeheart.

"Kepler, I ain't never been to no place but Brokeheart and Denver. I'm all scared, but I feel safe with you."

"It won't be easy. But you can make a new start. No one knows you where we're going."

She snuggled closer and shut her eyes. "Tell me 'gin the name of that place we're goin'."

I caught a strand of her hair in my fingers and touched my lips to her cheek.

"A town called Vengeance."

Acknowledgments

This author knows so well that a book is not so much the effort of an individual as it is the product of the encouragement, support, and faith of so many.

To the writer's critique group that has met in a coffee shop at Borders bookstore, then around tables at Panera's, and then in a corner at The Tattered Cover. Mary Ann, Liesa, ZJ, Mindy, Janet, Lizzie, Sue, Mike, Robin, Jess, Kathy, Ed, and the others, my thanks. I had a story–you taught me how to write it.

To Rocky Mountain Fiction Writers, who has the best writer's conference in the country, bar none. Thanks for teaching me the craft and business of becoming a writer.

To Gina Panettieri, the super agent who plucked this manuscript from her slush pile and believed in its writer. Thank you.

To my editor Reece Hanzon and the team at Jolly Fish Press. Thanks for hanging in despite the bumps along the way.

And to my proofreader, partner, and wife, Nancy. All my love.

About the Author

Kevin Wolf's debut novel, *The Homeplace,* is the winner of the 2015 Tony Hillerman Award. The great-grandson of Colorado homesteaders, Wolf enjoys fly-fishing, old Winchesters, 1950s Western movies, and the occasional bump in the night. He lives in Littleton, CO, with his wife and two beagles.

Previously Published:

The Homeplace: St Martin's Press (Minotaur) September 2016